Fatal Seduction

Fatal Cross Live!
Book 3

By
Theresa Hissong

Disclaimer:

This book is a work of fiction. Any resemblance to any person, living or dead is purely coincidental. The names of people, places, and/or things are all created from the author's mind and are only used for entertainment.

Due to the content, this book is recommended for adults 18 years and older.

Cover Design:
Custom eBook Covers

Editing by:
Heidi Ryan
Amour the Line Editing

Formatted by:
Wayne Hissong

Cover Model:
Stefan Northfield

Cover Photographer:
Eric Battershell

Other Books by Theresa Hissong

Fatal Cross Live!:
Fatal Desires
Fatal Temptations
Fatal Seduction

Rise of the Pride:
Talon
Winter
Savage
The Birth of an Alpha
Ranger

Book for Charity:
Fully Loaded

Dedication:

For those who've fought addiction and to those who are still finding their way out.

To Angela & Lynda:
You were strangers
to me,
but I will never forget
you.

Rest in Peace

Contents:

Prologue
Braxton
Remembering

The devil creeped through my blood, taking a part of me with him when I removed the needle from my vein. Delicious oblivion tickled my brain as my eyes rolled into the back of my head. The demon had become my best friend, being there for me in an instant, taking away the stresses in my life. I was learning that I couldn't live without him.

I didn't know how long I had passed out, but by the time I awoke, I was able to stagger to my feet and scoop up my keys from the table by the door.

That night was mostly a blur. My Abby was there in the car, her sweet scent swirled around me and was the only thing in my life that was pure anymore. I flinched when I noticed the scowl on her face, which led me to believe that she knew exactly what I'd been doing. Her eyes drifted to my arm, and I tried to bend it to keep her from seeing the marks that signaled my use like a bright beacon. When she voiced her thoughts, I knew she was more than pissed.

"Braxton," she gasped. "Are you doing heroin?"

"No," I growled, trying to blink the haze out of my eyes. I could feel the high slowly subsiding, and I wondered for a moment how much longer it would be

until I could be alone to get another fix. "Leave it alone, Abby."

"No," she snapped, her tiny hands reaching out to take my arm. "Damn it, Braxton! What have you done? Let me see them."

"Don't touch them!" I jerked my arm back as fear raced up my spine at the possibility of her fingers coming in contact with the poison that now owned my body. The last thing I wanted was Abby to touch the spot where I'd shot up, because the thought of her innocence being tainted by getting the drugs on her skin absolutely terrified me.

"Why, Braxton?" she cried, reaching for my arm again.

"Damn it, Abby! I said…SHIT!"

The steering wheel jerked to the left when I tried to yank away from her, forcing the tires to point toward the center median on the highway. I tried to correct, but it was too late.

Her screams were all around me, echoing through my mind. My own wounds were nothing…non-existent as I tried to move toward the sound of her voice, but I couldn't find her. No matter how hard I fought, no matter how hard I pushed my broken body to move, she was out of reach.

The smell of smoke and burning flesh surrounded me, making my stomach revolt. Strobing lights and sirens were the only things visible through the

darkness while her screams continued…my name falling from her lips.

There was one thing I would forever remember about that night…something that would haunt my dreams for the rest of my life.

Abby's voice as she screamed my name…

"Braxton!"

"Braxton!"

"Braxton! Please help me!"

Chapter 1
Braxton

I came awake with a hard jerk, sweat soaking the sheets underneath my body. I was tired of the nightmares…the dreams of her. I was haunted by guilt, and I doubted I would ever be free of that which plagued me.

Abby.

My Abby.

I'd taken something that was mine and destroyed it through my own stupidity. There had been times in my life where I'd done things I would always regret. Hell, all of us had that one thing we wished we could've changed; that one thing that kept you up at night as you tossed and turned, hoping you'd fall asleep before you slowly went insane.

Mine was the night I almost killed the woman who owned my heart, because I'd decided to drive after I'd stuck a needle in my arm to get high. My life would never be the same again, because it belonged to Abby…It'd always belong to Abby.

I only had the music to help me cope, but it would never help me forget my past.

Abagail Hampton, or Abby, as her friends and family called her, was the woman I saw when I used to daydream about my future plans. Still to this day, I could picture her long, blonde hair pulled up into a sloppy ponytail as she walked toward me with her hands resting protectively around her pregnant belly. I'd always had this dream of us, but now...that had changed into a living nightmare.

Now, my visions only included fire, crumpled metal, and her beautiful skin covered in burns.

Three years ago, I decided to pick her up after I'd gotten home from touring with my last band. I'd been partying nonstop for two months and had no plans on stopping. A few hours before I picked her up, I'd shot up and passed out, waking up to the sound of my phone ringing like crazy. I had managed to look presentable and, once I was done, I felt like I could at least pick up my girl and take her out to dinner.

The one thing I remembered from that night...the one thing that had stuck with me, were her screams and the fact that my legs were shattered. I was thrown from the car, and Abby was trapped inside when it caught fire. Her screams were incomparable to anything I had ever heard.

After I was released from the hospital, I was taken to jail for my crime. I was tried and given six months. I put myself into a drug treatment facility when I was released after only serving three months for good behavior. I completed the program, swearing I would never touch another illegal substance for as long as I lived.

During my stay in the hospital, I wrote Abby a letter, telling her I was letting her go. I couldn't even look her in the eye and pretend that everything was okay, and there was no way I could expect her forgiveness. My sister delivered the note, and when she returned, I was told that Abby was in a coma and her burns were severe. I think I actually died inside that day.

The one thing I did before I was put into jail was to have all of my worldly belongings sold and for my bank accounts to be changed over to a fund to pay for Abby's medical expenses. Her mother graciously accepted the offer, and I was told that Abby would not know that the money came from me. It was the least I could do.

Things changed shortly after that. I found a new band and a family in the three other men who shared my love of music. There was a bond there; one that was forged through our pasts. Each and every one of us had used drugs to the point it almost killed us. Even though our stories were different, we all knew the horrors of addiction.

I spent my nights touring and playing for thousands when I was alone inside. The music was my release, and the only way I knew how to survive what time I had left here on this earth. I yearned to forget Abby, but no matter how hard I've tried, she has been etched into my soul for all eternity. If things had been different, she would've been mine, and I would've cherished everything about her.

I heard Cora curse when she rushed past me to finish putting the final touches on our set. Presley was just coming off the stage when I finally got my shit together and made my way into the venue. Ace took his woman back toward the green room, and I stepped out of the way so I could stretch my arms, preparing them for the next hour.

Squeezing my eyes closed, I tried to push away the memories that haunted me. I'd lived the life of fast cars, heavy music, and drugs for too damn long. The past was always there; always reminding me of my failures against the woman I'd loved with my every breath. I wasn't sure if I would ever get to a point in my life where I would be able to forgive myself for almost killing her.

"You're on in five," Coraline said, reaching up to squeeze my shoulder. "You okay, Brax?"

"Yeah," I sighed. "I'm good. I'm ready for a break."

"Last show for a while." She smiled at me. "Go be a rockstar, my friend."

I grinned as she looped off toward the front of the stage. Coraline had come into our lives right when we had needed her most. Thankfully, Taylor had talked her into working for us, giving us a chance to tour without any worries.

She looked over her shoulder and gave me a thumbs up just as the lights went down. I didn't need a flashlight to find my kit, but Liam, one of our roadies, was there anyway, hunched down and out of sight.

"Ready when you are," he said, slipping away as I took my seat. I saw Ace, Taylor, and Cash waiting for my nod. It was time to play.

A bright flash of lights started the show. Ace jumped off the riser, growling out the beginning of the song as I beat out my frustrations on my kit. Well into the second song, one of my drumsticks broke. I quickly tossed it out into the crowd, scooping up a new one within a heartbeat. Sweat poured down the side of my neck as I continued to play, feeling the burn in my arms. Cash thrashed his head from side to side, making the women scream louder. His long hair covered his face, but that didn't hinder him from playing.

We moved through the first five songs and then started our current release. Ace screamed for all he was worth and the fans were slamming their bodies against each other as the music raised their adrenalin. Lights swirled around the stage and the crowd, lighting up faces in different colors. Coraline was sitting crossed-legged off to the side of the stage and behind a black curtain, watching us perform with Taylor aware of where she was at all times. Since she'd announced that they'd be having a child, he'd become even more protective of her, and I didn't blame him one bit.

The lights passed through the crowd as they swung wildly and with no real pattern, highlighting the faces of the fans. A split second before the venue went dark on the final song, my eyes zeroed in on a woman. My heart froze, and then began to gallop wildly in my chest. Her beautiful blonde hair fell around her shoulders, and I would know those dark blue eyes anywhere. I growled low in my throat as our gazes locked from across the venue floor. Her eyes widened when she realized I'd recognized her.

It was Abby.

My Abby.

And I was fucking pissed!

I stood from behind my kit, every ounce of blood in my body rolling through my veins like an out-of-control train. I heard Taylor curse when I jumped off the stage and into the crowd, my fists clenched at my sides. People moved out of my way as I stomped toward her. She was still standing as close as possible to the wall, her back pressed tightly against it so she was out of the way of people who were making their way toward the exit. I didn't stop until I was nose to nose with her.

"What the fuck are you doing here?"

"Well, hello to you, Braxton," she greeted, her voice barely above a whisper. Her scent washed over me, and I swayed where I stood from the rush of memories that flashed through my head. Memories of better times. "Is that any way to greet me after a year?"

God, had it been a year since the last time I'd seen her? She'd been in town when I was home from a tour and we'd bumped into each other. She tried to talk to me, but I made an excuse and walked away…just like I'd done all those years ago.

"Why are you here, Abby?" I pressed, looking around at the multitude of men watching her from the corner of their eyes. I wanted to beat them all within an inch of their lives. "This isn't the type of place for you."

"What?" she barked, her eyes narrowing. "Am I not allowed to go to a concert?"

"Fuck," I snarled, pinching the bridge of my nose. "What I mean is, what are you doing here alone?"

"I'm not alone," she smirked, placing a tiny hand on her right hip. "I came to see you."

"You know what I mean," I replied, finally taking in her appearance. She wore a shirt that carefully covered the scars on her arm, but left the damaged column of her neck exposed.

"I'm fine," she said, gritting her teeth. Her words were cut off when a few fans came up to shake my hand and ask for an autograph. I kept watch over her out of the corner of my eye, turning my body so she was protected from the small crowd that had gathered.

Ace, Cash, and Taylor spotted us as they came out from behind the stage with Cora and Liam escorting them to the front of the venue to sign some autographs. The fans that lingered in the building cheered and clapped as soon as they came into view. Ace's steps faltered when he got a look at who was behind me. He'd never met her, but had caught me looking at a picture of her a few weeks ago when I thought I was alone on the bus. I'd been so deep in thought, I didn't even hear him approach. Obviously, he remembered what she looked like from the photo.

"Brax?" Coraline frowned as she approached, casting a wary glance over my shoulder. Everyone stopped beside me, and Liam asked the crowd to go make a line out by the tables.

"Guys…" I swallowed, turning to the side. "This is Abby Hampton." I held my hand out toward her and watched as all of their eyes widened in recognition. Taylor was the first one to compose himself and step forward with an outstretched hand. Everyone introduced themselves, but Ace waited and watched her for a moment before approaching her, a soft smile on his face.

"I'm Ace," he said. "Nice to meet you, Abby."

"Hello." She smiled and looked up at me through her long lashes after she released his hand. "I need to talk to you, Braxton."

"Now isn't a good time, Abby," I lied. I really didn't want to talk to her. Talking to her put my head in a place that I didn't like…a place I'd worked so hard to avoid at all costs.

"When will be a good time, Braxton?" she snarled, her eyes narrowing. "It's been a year since I last saw you, and it's been *three years* since you left me in that hospital bed! Three years of avoiding me…avoiding *us*!"

"You need to leave," I growled, leaning over her so maybe, just maybe, I could intimidate her with my size, but she wasn't going to back down. I should've known that. Abigail Hampton wasn't easily pushed around, and that bratty side got her mouth into more trouble than necessary.

"Fuck that, Braxton Keller," she swore, taking her tiny hand and making a fist in my shirt. "I want to know why the hell you've been paying all of my medical bills!"

"You two need to get out of here," Ace said in a rush, taking my elbow and steering me away from the wall. "Take Abby in the back so you can talk."

"I have nothing to say," I warned, narrowing my eyes on her. She didn't need an explanation. No one needed an explanation for the things I did.

"Well, I do," she said, crossing her arms over her chest. I didn't even look at what that did to her breasts. I wouldn't let her distract me.

"Now," Ace ordered, giving me one last push.

"Come on," I mumbled, taking her by her uninjured arm. I didn't drag her, but she did have to take faster steps to keep up with my longer strides.

"I'm not a child, Braxton," she huffed, jerking her arm away. When I turned my head to glare at her, she narrowed her eyes but wisely kept her mouth shut.

"But I see you're still a brat," I mumbled, pushing open the backstage doors.

Chapter 2
Abby

My Abby,

I will never be able to forgive myself for what I have done to you. It kills me to let you go, but I have done things that I will have to live with for the rest of my life.

You deserve happiness with someone who will treat you like a princess.

I don't know if you will ever be able to forgive me for the things I've done, but I hope in time that you can.

Braxton

I folded the worn letter carefully and ran the tip of my finger across where my name had been written in black ink. That letter had been sitting in my nightstand for the past three years. It'd been opened and closed so many times, there were weak spots in the creases, leaving tiny holes announcing that it wouldn't stay together much longer.

It was the letter Braxton had sent to me after I was hospitalized from the wreck that scarred my body. The wreck he caused the night he decided to drive high on heroin.

We'd been together for two years before that fateful night, our relationship surviving during his time on the road with his old band, but that night was different.

He'd been home for a few days and he'd picked me up for a night out, but he was acting strange. I questioned him and received a hateful answer. I kept my mouth closed, but after he got on the highway, he began to swerve. I originally thought he was drunk, but with one shift of his arm, I saw it…the marks that gave away the life he'd lived on the road.

When I confronted him, he got angry, screaming at me to leave him alone. He took his hands off of the steering wheel just long enough to lose control of the car, crashing into the concrete barriers that divided the highway.

And that was all I remembered.

I woke in the hospital. My leg was burned from my hip to my knee, my ribs, and my left arm from my shoulder to the back of my hand. Those bothered me the most…still a constant reminder of that night.

I'd seen him only once since he left town to go into a drug rehab program. A year ago, we'd crossed paths not long after he had found a place with his current band, *Fatal Cross*. I was happy for him, because he was chasing his dreams and thriving as the drummer of the hottest up-and-coming band in the business. Tonight, I would see him for the first time in just over a year.

I pulled my blonde hair over my left shoulder, using it as a curtain to hide the scars on my neck. The blouse I wore was a convertible, one-shoulder black top that was long sleeved on my left side and was missing a sleeve on the other. The black material swooped off of my shoulder and the elastic band kept it nice and tight under my armpit on my unscarred side. My jeans were faded and tight, and on my feet were a pair of heels that would make a movie star jealous.

I slid the silver bangles on my wrists and dabbed just a small amount of perfume on my neck. I winced when my elbow protested, reminding me of the recent surgery to remove the scar tissue and repair some tendons and ligaments that had been bothering me for the past six months.

Tonight, I wasn't going to think about that any more than I had to, because I was tired of fucking thinking about when I would be able to live my life without pain or the reminders of the night that changed my life. I squared my shoulders and dusted my nose with powder. One last peek in the mirror, and I was ready to go.

My apartment was in downtown Seattle, not far from the venue. I decided to take a cab for the five mile journey instead of taking my car. I wasn't planning on drinking tonight, but sometimes being a woman alone in a parking lot just wasn't the smartest idea on a Friday night after a rock concert.

The cab driver took my money as I exited the car, and his appreciative glance at my body didn't go unnoticed. People were lined up down the sidewalk in front of the building, waiting for the doors to open. I walked down the line, looking for the end to take my place. A few men stared at me as I passed. I didn't dare look at them, because in all honesty, I was scared shitless.

This wasn't my usual hangout. Usually, I preferred the library or a bookstore with the smell of freshly brewed coffee. The past three years, I didn't get out much, because I really didn't have any friends that stuck around after the accident. I didn't hold a grudge, either. They had their lives, too, and my months of rehabilitation got in the way of going out for dinner and drinks and even concerts.

The line moved slowly as the doors were opened. It took about fifteen minutes before I reached the entrance. The big guy at the door checked my driver's license and took the small portion of my ticket stub before waving me through.

As I entered the main area of the venue, I noticed that the walls were painted black and there was minimal lighting where the audience would be standing. There were no seats, except up next to two bars at the back of the room.

Men and women walked around, most of them sporting shirts for various bands. Several of them wore shirts showing their love for *Fatal Cross*, making me smile. I'd been a fan of the band since before Braxton had joined them.

A local band opened the show, spending about thirty minutes on stage before the lights went down. I grabbed myself a drink at the bar and made my way closer to the stage. I stood off to the right, allowing other people to cram close to the stage to see the next band to perform. I was rather shy around strangers and didn't want to get caught up in anything wild like a mosh pit.

The next band was really good, and I'd heard one of their songs on the radio just a few days before the show. The lead singer was female and she had a set of pipes on her that could shoot that band into stardom before the year was up.

As the night progressed, I started wondering if maybe I should've just stayed home. If he saw me, I knew Braxton was going to be pissed off. He didn't want me anywhere near him, and my stupid attempt of showing up at his concert was probably one of the dumbest ideas I'd ever had, but I had to see him. If he did see me and I was able to have a word with him, there was something that needed to be said to his face. I had to steel my spine and keep to my plan. It was too late to back out now, the lights were going down and *Fatal Cross* was heading to the stage. I wiped my sweaty hands on my jeans and prayed he didn't see me. Maybe I could watch him play and then sneak out before the show ended.

Boy was I ever wrong…

As soon as the lights went up, I saw him for the first time in what seemed like forever. My heart thundered in my chest when I saw just how huge he had gotten since the last time I'd seen him. He'd gained so much muscle in the last three years, he looked like he weighed twice as much as he did before the accident. His body was covered with tattoos, and little beads of sweat were making an appearance on his forehead as he played the first song.

Not only had he changed, but his eyes were not the vibrant blue that they once were. In them, I saw pain, and that alone ripped my heart to shreds because I knew I was the one that had caused his guilt.

One song bled into the next, and I found myself bobbing my head to each one the lead singer was belting out to his fullest. The band's guitarist was jumping around on stage, acting his part. The bassist looked like every woman's fantasy with his long, blond hair. A few women in the crowd screamed when he'd wink at them.

The lights began to pulse and Braxton was pounding out a beat that matched the lights. The crowd screamed and the next song began. A woman stumbled into me, and I smiled as she righted herself with a slurred apology. I watched as she made her way to the restrooms, disappearing in the door marked for women.

As the last song came to a close, I felt a pain in my chest. It would probably be the last time I saw him. I moved to my left so I could have one last clear look at the man who held my heart no matter what he'd done.

White lights blinked once, twice, and on the third time, I saw him.

Braxton Keller's eyes locked with mine and a split second later, I saw recognition in his hard gaze. He'd seen me, but I was frozen in place as he stood from his drum kit. His shoulders seemed to double in size as he moved forward on the stage. The crowd gasped, parting in a rush when he made a leap from the stage to the venue floor. He didn't care that there were hundreds of people crammed into the area…he just walked forward like a man on a mission. His eyes hardened, and I took a step back, but didn't get far because the wall met my back.

I was stuck there like prey in the scope of a rifle…the hunter poised and ready to fire. I was trapped by the man who'd scarred me…the man who'd changed my life forever.

* * *

I was currently sitting with my ass parked in a metal folding chair somewhere behind the stage. Braxton was pacing. I rolled my eyes and opened my mouth. "You pace too much when you're stressed. Stop it."

He froze and looked over his shoulder, his eyes going dark. The muscles in his jaw ticced, and I could probably bounce a quarter off the tightness.

"Abby, you're being a brat," he warned. His hand twitched and I remembered when he used to paint my ass red for my wayward mouth. I had to stifle a moan.

"I have every right to be," I said, standing up from my seat. I wanted to be on the same level with him. "Why are you paying my bills? I have insurance."

"You know why," he mumbled, turning away from me. I saw the answer in his eyes before he started pacing again.

"Because of your guilt?" I tossed that at him just to see how he'd react. He spun with a hard jerk.

"Yes!" he yelled, stepping up so he was looming over me, but I'd never been afraid of Braxton Keller. He could try to bully me all he wanted, but I was stronger than he thought. I also had a stubborn streak a mile wide. "Because it was my carelessness that caused your scars…caused you to be hurt, Abby."

"Did you ever think that part of that accident was my fault, too?" I sucked in a breath when his eyes turned almost black. Oh, he was pissed.

"Seriously?" he scoffed.

"If I'd kept my mouth shut, you wouldn't have lost control of the car, Braxton," I replied, knowing he wasn't going to accept my statement.

"I was high, Abby!" He ran his hands through his short, cropped brown hair, the muscles in his arm flexing with the movement. He'd changed a lot in three years. He wasn't below-average size anymore, and his body was now covered in tattoos. I was sure each and every one of them had a story, and I was afraid to look deeper into each piece, worried I'd find a lot of them were reminders of what had happened.

"I forgave you the moment I woke up in the hospital," I stated, knowing that probably wasn't the best thing to say to him.

"Well, I haven't forgiven myself," he whispered, wiping a hand down his face.

"We need to talk, Braxton." I sighed, looking around at the backstage area. "Here isn't the place."

"I really don't want to talk about this," he snarled. His attitude was just starting to piss me off, but I knew from experience that he was one of the most hardheaded men on the face of the planet. "Let me call you a cab."

"No, thanks," I scoffed. "I'm capable of taking care of myself, Braxton. I've been doing it for three years." I knew slinging more guilt wasn't the greatest idea when dealing with him, but he needed to understand that I wasn't as fragile as he believed.

"You are not walking home from here," he stated.

"No, I'm not walking. I can also get my own cab," I barked as I pushed past him and made my way out of the backstage area. "I thought I could come here and have an adult conversation with you, but it looks like I was wrong."

"Wait," he called out, running a tattooed hand through his hair. When I turned around, his jaw was set and I noticed a tic that told me he was angry. I knew that look, but like before, it didn't faze me.

"So, are we talking or not?"

"Yes, I have been paying your bills," he began, but paused when some people entered the door from the front of the venue. They ignored us and moved along quickly. "There will be no arguing about this, Abby."

"Again, I have insurance, Braxton," I huffed. "I really wish you'd stop."

"That's not going to happen," he barked out a harsh laugh. "Ever."

"You are so stubborn," I said, throwing my hand in the air; the good hand that didn't hurt when I moved it too quickly. Right then, I really wanted to use both of them to strangle him.

"I'll call you a cab," he said, making a move to walk away. I reached out and placed my hand on his arm and felt the familiar warmth of his skin. We both froze as I swallowed hard and looked at where my hand was touching him. For a split second, it felt like old times, like home, but with a jerk of his arm, the connection was lost.

"Okay," I replied, and followed him out to the curb where a cab was already waiting.

Chapter 3
Braxton

The scent of dust and musty furniture burned my nose when I pushed the door to my apartment wide open. Nothing had changed since I'd left a few months ago. The small one-bedroom apartment was all I needed. Hell, it was all I wanted.

I dropped my bag on the couch and made my way into the kitchen. A note sat on my small table, folded into a silly teepee. I avoided it while I checked out what was in my fridge. The cool air caused bumps to raise on my skin when I pulled the door open. The thing was full of food, and I shook my head at my mother's overly excessive shopping.

I grabbed a glass and poured myself some water from the gallon jug in the door. The chair creaked when I sat down and picked up the piece of paper from the table. It was from my sister.

Braxton,
Food is in the fridge. You need to call me as soon as you get in so we can go to mom's house for a family dinner.

Don't stay in this God awful apartment for the next two weeks!

I will come drag you out…this is your only warning.

Love you, Bubba!

Penny

My baby sister, Penelope, was only my baby sister by two and a half minutes, but she always watched over me as if she was the one older. Having a twin was sometimes a blessing…other times it was a pain in my ass.

I ignored the phone when it rang and found my way into my bathroom. It took me twenty minutes to shower and shave, and by the time I left the bedroom, my phone was screaming again.

"What is it, Penny?" I barked into the phone. "I just got home."

"Braxton Andrew Keller," she scolded. "Is that anyway to talk to your sister?"

I wiped my hand down my face and took a deep breath, knowing I shouldn't be an asshole, but I'd just seen the woman that I'd almost killed, and she wanted to remind me of my past by showing up looking like a walking wet dream.

"I'm sorry," I replied.

"What's wrong?" she whispered. Another thing about having a twin was that we had this crazy connection. Penny was always better at reading my moods than I was at deciphering hers.

"Abby showed up at the show last night," I admitted, squeezing my eyes closed as I tried to get her face out of my head.

There was a pause on the other end of the line, then a heavy sigh. "Braxton, you need to talk to her."

"I have nothing to say to her," I replied, making a fist on the table top. "I'm sure my almost killing her cured her of any feelings she had for me."

"What did Abby say last night at the show?" Penny pushed.

I explained everything, down to me rushing from the stage like a raging bull. There was no way that Abby wanted anything to do with me, except to rub in my face that her scars were my fault.

"I still think you two need to sit down and talk everything out, Brax," Penny urged. "I'm serious. It's the only way you are going to move past this…this guilt."

"Penelope," I warned, using her full name.

"Do it, Braxton," she ordered. "I mean it…and be at mom's tomorrow night at six."

Before I could reply, she hung up the phone, leaving me sitting in my shady ass apartment all alone.

Times like these were when the cravings came rushing back. It'd been just over three years since that fateful night and the last time I ever stuck a needle in my arm, but damn if I still didn't want the high when my guard was down. I didn't know if I'd ever completely lose the desire for it, either. The only thing that kept me from going out to find the drugs was remembering her screams. That would cure me of any craving I had for the poison that ruled my life and almost destroyed it.

A thump outside caught my attention. Someone was walking up the stairs toward my apartment. The way the building was set up, the stairs from below only reached toward the apartment above the bottom one and stopped on a landing outside my door and front window.

I saw her silhouette before she knocked.

"How the fuck did she find me?"

It didn't take long for the answer to hit me like a freight train…Penny.

"Fuck," I growled, standing up from my seat.

Chapter 4
Abby

I knew coming here would be a bad idea, but I just couldn't take no for an answer. His sister, Penny, had become my dearest friend over the past three years. She understood her brother better than anyone else, and she knew that his avoiding me was because of what happened to me all those years ago.

Since he was in town, I finally had a chance to convince him that he needed to quit holding all of this guilt over the accident. He wanted to take all of the blame, but even though I was the one with the most traumatic injuries, I still knew what happened to me that night. It would be hard to convince him, but I was determined to at least get us back on speaking terms. The fact that I still loved him, no matter what had happened, would probably go with me to my grave.

"What are you doing here?" he growled, not opening the door all the way. Braxton leaned his arm against the door frame, his tattoos flexing with the tension in his muscles. I didn't miss the way his eyes heated as his gaze traveled down my body. I knew I affected him, and I hoped he could look past my scars long enough for me to remind him how good things used to be.

"I came to talk to you," I replied, holding my chin high. I wouldn't look intimidated on the outside, but on the inside, I was shaking like a lone leaf in a hurricane.

"Go home, Abby," he ordered, but I wasn't backing down. "This isn't a good neighborhood."

"About that, Braxton," I said, gritting my teeth. "Why the hell are you living in a rundown apartment?" I knew the answer to that. He was spending thousands and thousands on my medical care and had nothing left for himself. That shit was going to end real fast.

"That's none of your business," he grunted.

"The hell it isn't, Braxton," I barked, pushing my body forward. I was surprised when he stepped back, allowing me to walk inside. What I found there almost brought me to tears.

The apartment was half the size of my own. His looked like nothing more than a studio with a fake wall to partition off the bedroom. It was a square with a living space on my left and a small kitchen table to my right. If you broke it down into four corners, you would place the bedroom in number one, the kitchen in number two, the living room in number three, and the eating area in number four.

Shades that darkened the room hung haphazardly from the window that looked out over the landing in front of his door. Only a small lamp was lit on a wooden crate next to an old brown couch. The entire apartment looked like it belonged to a person who barely made ends meet, not a drummer for one of the biggest up-and-coming bands in the industry.

"Please, Braxton, talk to me," I pleaded, folding my arms across my chest. I winced slightly when I felt the pull on my stitches from the surgery I'd just had to release a tendon in my elbow. It wasn't a huge surgery, it was more for maintenance on the spot where I'd had the most severe burns.

"Abby," Braxton gasped, moving to my side. His hands stilled as he reached out to touch me. "Why are you out of the house? You need to be resting after your surgery." I knew the moment he realized he'd just let his secret out of the bag by the way he froze, his eyes narrowing dangerously.

"I'm fine." I pulled away from him and moved to take a seat at the kitchen table, but he didn't follow. He propped his beefy shoulder against the small partition leading to his bedroom.

"What did the doctor say?" he asked, his voice softening.

"The surgery went very well," I replied, my voice trailing off into a frustrated growl when I realized he was changing the subject. "I didn't come here to talk about me."

"Well, we sure as fuck are not going to talk about me," he exploded, running his tattooed hand through his short-cropped brown hair. The thick muscle in his jaw ticced as his eyes narrowed. "Abby, you can't be here. I…I just can't be around you. It hurts too much."

"Do I disgust you now?" I asked, my voice barely above a whisper. That was the one thing I didn't want to happen. If he looked at me in that way, I would leave. I didn't want him to think I was a freak.

"God, no!" he gasped, taking a knee before me. "You are even more beautiful than I remember."

"Then why, Braxton?" I asked, tears welling up in my eyes. "Tell me why you have avoided me. Be honest…please?"

"The songs I write? They're all about you!" he growled, rising to his feet to pace.

"Braxton…" I began, but he cut me off with a slash of his tattooed hand. The agony on his face brought more tears to my eyes. Before I could say or do anything, he moved forward so quickly it startled me, but when he raised his hands, cupping my face, I knew whatever he had to say was something I needed to hear. The tight hold hurt for a second until he realized his touch was too much.

"Abby, I hear you screaming in my nightmares," he admitted, his voice cracking as he spoke. "I can still smell your flesh as it burned…still hear you calling for me to save you. I live with this guilt, and I will never be the same man as I was before I stuck a fucking needle in my arm and drove that car."

"Braxton," I choked out, pushing his hands away from my face. He rose to his feet as I did, and took a step back. I moved closer to him to be on a more even level, even if that meant I was still six inches shorter. He only stilled when my hand rested on his arm. We both looked at the contact, and I noticed the scars on the back of my hand. I jerked it away quickly and continued, "I don't blame you. Hell, I *never* blamed you."

"I blame myself, and that's why I had to let you go." He sighed, glancing at my hand again.

"Do you understand me? I cannot love you anymore, because how in the hell could you love me after what I did?"

"Braxton, look at me," I said softly. When he raised his eyes, I could see all of his pain and it punched me right in my heart. "I've never stopped loving you."

Time froze as his face fell and his eyes widened at my confession. The tension in the room thickened like an invisible fog. I knew the moment the words I'd spoken registered, because his face turned bright red with his anger.

"You need to leave," he demanded. "Now, Abby!"

I waited all of two minutes for him to say he was sorry. Maybe even reach out for me, but all he did was stare at me as if he were in a trance. *Maybe I shouldn't have said that.*

"I…I'll go," I whispered, and grabbed my bag. When I turned around to look at him one last time, Braxton still hadn't moved from his spot.

Chapter 5
Braxton

"Oh, son," my mother cooed as she met me at the door. I didn't want to come here, but I knew my sister would've showed up at my place to drag me out if I didn't. "I'm so glad you're home."

"Me too, Mama," I said, wrapping my arms around her.

She smelled like home…like simpler times. I let her squeeze me for several minutes, honestly not caring if she held on for longer. What was it about a mother's embrace that made all of your worries fade away? Fuck, I was such a pussy. Twenty-seven and still relied on my mother to chase away the bad shit in my head.

"It's about time you showed up," Penny snarled as she found me in the foyer, still hugging my mom. I kissed my mother's temple and backed away, accepting another hug from my twin.

"Jesus, Penny," I gasped, wrapping my hand around her upper arm. "Have you been eating anything?" She looked thin…too thin.

"I'm not a meathead like you," she huffed, sticking her tongue out and spinning on her heel. "I haven't changed any. You've just gotten bigger." Yeah, I was going to have to watch her. I didn't like the way she looked at all.

"Come into the kitchen, I need you to put the steaks on the grill, son," my mother ordered. One thing about my mom, she was as sweet as could be, but when she gave an order, you obeyed…even if you were a grown-ass man.

I held my hands out for the platter and waited for Penny to open the slider to the deck. I shivered when the cold wind bit at my face. Seattle wasn't anywhere near as inviting as most of the places I'd traveled to, but it was my home, and I didn't want to be anywhere else.

As soon as I entered the kitchen, my mom dropped the towel on the counter that she was using to wipe her hands. She handed me a bowl of potatoes and pushed me toward the table, following me with one of her own. I turned around and took that one from her, placing the vegetables in their place.

We worked quietly for the next twenty minutes until the steaks were done. I placed the platter on the table and took my seat at the head where my father used to sit. My mother had insisted that I was to take his place after he passed away. I didn't feel like the man of the family anymore, but I did as my mother wished, because I was still respectful.

"So, tell me about the tour?" she asked, passing the platter toward my sister.

"It was great," I grunted as I tucked into my food. "The crowds are getting bigger."

"I've been seeing a lot of photos and articles on the internet." Penny smiled, but her face sobered. "You deserve this, Brax."

"Thank you," I replied, but froze when her tiny hand landed on my forearm. "What?"

"We need to talk about it," she urged, giving me a knowing look.

"Penny," I growled in warning. "Not now."

"Then when?" my mother asked, dropping her fork next to her plate. "I'm sorry, Braxton, but it *kills* me to see you like this. You used to be so happy and outgoing. Now, all you do is mope around and never speak about anything."

"Why are you both ganging up on me?" I barked, feeling like shit when my mother flinched. "Fuck, Ma. I'm sorry."

"Language, Braxton Keller," she scolded.

"Yes, ma'am," I said in defeat.

"We are just worried about you." Penny finally spoke up after a few minutes of awkward silence. "You've changed so much."

"I'm not doing drugs," I answered, "if that's what you're thinking." Why were they doing this? I wasn't doing anything wrong.

"I know you are not." My mom sighed loudly. "Your worrying about Abby is slowly killing you, Braxton. This needs to stop."

"I will always worry about her," I growled, setting my napkin beside my plate. "I'll clean up the dishes."

"Sit your ass down," my mom snarled, causing me to freeze. My mother never cursed. "I'm not done speaking with you."

"Damn," I mumbled under my breath. "Do we really have to do this now?"

"When will be a good time, Braxton?" my mom pushed. "Next year? The year after? When?"

"How about never?" I suggested, knowing she wasn't going to stand down.

"Not going to happen," Penny smirked. I assumed now that they had me cornered, my mother and sister were going to voice their opinions on my behavior.

Boy, was I ever right.

"She still loves you," Penny announced, but she didn't have to say it. I already knew. I could see it in the way she looked at me after the concert and when she showed up on my doorstep.

"You still love her," my mom said. By no means was that a question. She was stating a fact; a fact that everyone around me knew more so than I did.

"How could I not love her?" I asked, shaking my head.

"Then go to her, work things out," Penny urged. "You're going to be home for a few weeks. It would probably help you if you two at least talked things out. You never had the chance to do that after the accident."

"No, I didn't," I grumbled. "I was in jail."

"You could've gone to her as soon as you got out," mom reminded me. "You are the one who put the self-imposed restraining order on yourself, Braxton. Not her."

I sat there in silence, letting all of their words sink in, but my own guilt always outweighed everything when it came to Abby. It was almost like that demon was still sitting on my shoulder, making my life a living hell.

Chapter 6
Abby

I thumbed through the racks of clothes, really not paying much attention to what I was looking at. I couldn't shake the knowledge that Braxton was still suffering over the things that had happened. He may have looked different from when we'd been together, but inside, he was still the same. Inside, he really cared.

Penny shuffled along beside me quietly. I already knew she wanted to ask me about Braxton, but I didn't have the answers she was looking for. Occasionally, I'd catch her looking at me from the corner of her eye, but she never voiced what she wanted to say.

"Oh, just spill it," I sighed. "It's killing you to ask me, isn't it?"

"Did you go by his place?" she finally asked, biting her lip. Even though Penny and Braxton were fraternal twins, they had the same mannerisms and movements. The little ticks, like biting their bottom lip, was so similar it was scary.

"Yes," I answered, pulling a shirt out to look at it thoroughly. "Do you think this would look good on me?"

"Yes." She frowned. "Tell me what happened with my brother."

"Nothing." I blew out a breath, making my bangs fly up and settle back on my forehead. "He basically kicked me out."

"He did what?" She yelled so loud, two elderly ladies jumped from the sound. I narrowed my eyes at her when she spit out an offhanded, "I'm sorry," to the ladies.

"That wasn't nice, Penny," I scolded.

"I'm going to kill him," she mumbled.

"You will do no such thing," I warned. "Let me handle Braxton."

"Good luck with that," she laughed, loudly.

We shopped for another hour, leaving the store to pursue a place to grab lunch. Our choices were plentiful, but we ended up settling on a small pizza place not far from the store. When we entered, I noticed two men sitting at a table in the corner. Their eyes roamed both of our bodies and one of them gave Penny a wink. She rolled her eyes and walked to the counter to order her food.

"Jerks," she said under her breath.

Penny was stunningly beautiful. Her hair was the exact same dark brown as Braxton's, but hers fell in waves to her waist. She wore makeup like a professional and had the body of a movie star.

"Quit pulling at your sleeves," she whispered. I hadn't even realized I was tugging at the three-quarter sleeve top she'd insisted I wear. It was hot outside, but I liked my long sleeves to cover the scars. Penny told me I shouldn't hide who I was, but I couldn't take that step and wear something any shorter than what I was currently wearing.

"Sorry, habit," I said, stepping up to place my order. "Just a slice of cheese pizza and a water, please."

The young man behind the counter smiled warmly at me and took my money, handing over the receipt and promising to bring the food out shortly. Penny steered me toward the other side of the restaurant, finding a small table for us to use away from the two gawking men.

"Those guys are making me nervous." I said after the waiter brought our food. They finished their meal shortly after we were seated, but they didn't leave.

One was probably in his mid-thirties with dark brown hair that reached his shoulders. The other was slightly younger with jet black hair.

Both of them looked like they needed a shower and maybe some new clothes.

Penny took a bite of her pizza and nodded for me to start eating. I raised my eyebrow in question when I saw her shoot off a text message on her phone. She shook her head and took a sip of her drink. "It's going to be okay."

"Who did you text?" I asked, knowing in the back of my mind that it was probably her brother.

"Eat," she demanded, taking another bite of her food.

We both ate a little faster than usual; our conversations were at a minimum. I wiped the corner of my mouth and set my napkin to the side just as I noticed Penny sitting up straighter in her seat and freezing.

"Hello, ladies," the dark haired one announced as he approached the table. "What are a couple of beauties like you doing today? Can we join you?"

"Nope," Penny shot off. Her eyes flared with anger as she turned in her seat. "We were just trying to have some lunch...alone."

"Pretty ladies like you shouldn't be alone," the other man snickered, grabbing a chair from the table behind us. He straddled the thing backwards and leaned his dirty arms on the back. "What's your name?"

"That's really none of your business, now is it?" Penny continued. "I'd also ask that you move. I never gave you an invitation to sit with us."

"Come on now, sugar," the first one drawled, his eyes heating as they roamed her body.

"What about you, blondie?" the second one asked, turning his eyes on me. "What say you and I go out for a little dessert?"

"That would be a negative," I replied, rolling my eyes. "I'm full from lunch."

"I don't think you're quite full enough," he suggested, reaching out to touch my arm…the one that was scarred and recently operated on.

"Stop!" Penny yelled as his hand clamped down on my elbow. I gasped out in pain from his hard grip. One second, the man was holding my arm…and the next, he was flying. When I looked up at my savior, all of the air whooshed from my lungs.

Braxton was standing there, his eyes dark with anger. The moment he turned to go after the man, Penny jumped from her seat. I was in too much pain to beg him not to cause a scene, but it was too late.

"Braxton, stop!" Penny warned, putting her body between her brother and the two men. "You can't do this."

I knew what she was saying. Braxton already had a record, and having the cops called on him wouldn't look good. He needed to stay out of trouble.

"Braxton," I whispered, not knowing if he heard me or not. My voice wasn't audible enough for anyone to really hear me. The pain in my arm was severe, and I knew I wasn't going to be able to shake this one off. My butt hit the chair as I pulled my arm close to my body. I leaned over slightly to try and put pressure over the damage.

The two men stood up from their places on the ground. I didn't think they realized until they started after Braxton that he was as big as both of them combined. They took one look at him and backed out of the restaurant.

"Abby," he gasped as he turned around, dropping to his knees next to me. The man whom I loved more than life itself hovered protectively as his eyes zeroed in on me. "Where are you hurt?"

"He grabbed my arm," I hissed as the pain flared. "I'll be okay. I just need to go home and lay down. I think I'm going to need one of my pain pills."

"You're going to my place," he said matter-of-factly, standing to his full height. "You both are."

Penny didn't put up much of a fuss. She just cleaned our table as Braxton stood there staring at me. I didn't need him getting angry, or even yelling. So, I stood up and brushed past him on my way to the door. I didn't need to look back to see if he was following me. His heavy footsteps were a clear indicator that he wasn't far away.

"You're riding with me," he stated, taking my uninjured elbow in his firm grip. It wasn't too hard, but it wasn't gentle, either. I knew better than to argue with him that I'd rather ride with Penny. I just kept my mouth shut and slid into the passenger side of his truck when he opened the door.

Chapter 7
Braxton

The text I received sent my heart plummeting to my feet. My sister had only said I needed to come to the pizza place down the road from my apartment and to hurry. What I found when I walked inside boiled my blood as it ran through my veins.

Those two men were harassing them and one of them had touched my Abby. He'd actually brought her pain and that was not sitting well with me at all. If it wasn't for my sister placing a calming hand on my chest, I would've killed them.

"Do you have your medicine?" I growled, knowing I sounded pissed beyond reason, but I wasn't mad at her. I was just mad at the situation.

"In my bag," she whispered, nodding toward her purse on the floorboard of my truck.

"Take what you need, and then you can stay at my place until you are better," I offered, gritting my teeth at the end, because having her in my apartment was a bad idea.

"Can you just take me home?" she asked, screwing her nose up as if she'd smelled something bad. It was probably my attitude.

"No," I replied blankly. "I need to make sure you're okay."

"I'll be fine, Brax," she said.

"Don't argue with me," I barked.

"Fine," she huffed, reaching into her bag and retrieving the pills. I didn't say anything, because I knew she needed them. I hated manmade drugs...hell, I hated all drugs. After dealing with Ace and his back injury, I understood the need for them when the person was in pain, but I didn't like what they did to a person's body in the long run.

Penny pulled into the visitor's parking spot next to my truck and hopped out of her car, coming to the passenger side to help Abby out and up the stairs to my apartment. I was right behind them as we reached the landing. I kept silent as I unlocked the door and threw it open wide enough for both of the girls to get inside. As soon as my foot cleared the door, I turned and locked the deadbolt, ensuring none of the scum in my neighborhood could get inside. I had too much precious cargo in my home to take a chance.

"Do you want to lay down?" Penny asked as they approached the couch.

"Just for a little while," Abby yawned. The pills were obviously working.

"Braxton, grab her a blanket and extra pillow, please," my sister ordered. I wasted no time in finding the softest blanket I had and the best, fluffiest pillow I could find.

Abby sighed heavily as she settled in when I placed the pillow down on the arm of my long couch, closing her eyes as soon as she was comfortable. I took a seat in my small kitchen, watching as she slowly fell into a deep slumber. When I looked up, Penny was sitting across from me, watching my every move.

"Thank you," she said, running a hand through her long, brown hair.

"Why were you out in this part of town, anyway?" I prodded.

"We were shopping at the clothing store we like and decided that the pizza place was fine for lunch," she answered, rolling her eyes. "I shop that store all the time and sometimes stop for pizza there, Braxton. This never happens to me."

"You scared me to death," I growled, trying my hardest not to be loud and wake up Abby.

"I'm sorry, Braxton." She frowned. "Seriously. If I thought it was dangerous, you know I wouldn't have gone there."

"I know you wouldn't have," I relented, standing up and pulling her from the chair. I hugged my sister tightly and closed my eyes. They could've been seriously hurt.

"Can you take Abby home when she's feeling better?" she asked, pushing away from me. "I need to go home and get ready for tomorrow."

"It's your big day, huh?" I teased, ruffling her hair. "You'll do fine."

"If I don't faint on set from the nerves," she laughed, grabbing her keys. "See ya."

Penny had landed a role in a new movie that was being filmed in our home town. She'd been acting since she was eighteen and was doing pretty good for herself. She wasn't vastly popular yet, but I was confident she would get there soon.

My sister had gone through so much growing up. Her weight had always bothered her, and I watched her like a hawk since we'd found out that she'd been making herself throw up every morsel of food she'd ingested.

It'd been several years since she'd gone through a program and learned to eat healthy and exercise. I'd been concerned when I came home and found her about fifteen pounds lighter than when I'd left on tour. She acted okay, and I hadn't seen anything that would lead me to believe she was falling back into that hole again.

Abby made a noise as she moved in her sleep, bringing me back from my memories. I walked over toward the couch and took a seat on the ground after pulling the blanket up over her shoulders.

She hadn't changed in all of this time. My Abby was still as beautiful as the day I first met her five years ago. The only change was her matured features and the scars on her body. Those were my fault and would always be something that haunted me day and night.

My phone chimed with an incoming text. The guys wanted to get together the next night to practice at the warehouse space we owned in Seattle, and I needed the distraction. A good four hour session behind my kit was just what the doctor ordered.

Looking over my shoulder and seeing Abby there, nestled on my couch, sent my heart back into that dark place that seemed more like a home than a hindrance. I couldn't keep her. She wasn't mine anymore.

She had this fantasy that things would go back to the way they had been. I knew this, because I could see it in her eyes. If I was honest with myself, I'd say that I wanted that as well. Reality and life were nothing but a hateful bitch, and I knew it would never work out between us. It hurt too much to look at her.

As soon as she woke from her nap, I would take her home and prepare for our next tour. That was the only option. She couldn't keep coming around me. It just wasn't fair to either one of us.

I loved her...but I had to let her go.

Chapter 8
Abby

My eyes blinked slowly as I woke up. At first, I wasn't sure where I was, but it wasn't long before I realized I had been asleep on Braxton's couch. The scent of him was all around me, and I didn't want to think about the fact that it was more than likely in my clothes.

"I need to take you home," Braxton announced as I sat up. He was across the tiny room, sitting in a chair at his kitchen table. His eyes were on me, but they were unfocused, like his mind was a million miles away. I didn't like that look in his eyes.

He wore a pair of black denim jeans. There were tears and rips in them that obviously came from the manufacturer. His cut up concert shirt, showing some band I'd never heard of, draped over his massive chest. The multitude of tattoos that covered his arms drew my attention and I traced each line and color with my eyes. I saw the muscles in his arm flex as my gaze traveled to his thick neck.

"You can't look at me like that," he warned.

"Why not?" I asked, clearing my throat. "You used to like it when I would look at you."

"Things have changed, Abby," he replied, standing up from his seat. He reached behind him and picked up my bag. "Penny had to go home. I will take you over to your place."

"I can call a cab," I gritted out through clenched teeth.

"No," he replied. "I want to make sure you are safe at home."

"Fine," I snapped, climbing to my feet.

I pushed past him as he stood off to the side of the door. My hand grazed his hip and I heard him groan low under his breath. The only solace I had was he was still obviously affected by me.

"I'm assuming you know where I live," I accused, my words clipped with my anger. "Since you know where the medical bills come."

"Not now, Abby," he grumbled.

I sat back in the seat and folded my arms across my chest, mindful of my healing elbow.

The ride to my place only took twenty minutes. I wanted to storm up to my apartment and slam the door like a child, but I didn't. As soon as he put his truck into park, I opened the door, blinking when the interior lights illuminated the inside of the truck. I didn't even look at him as I climbed out. "Have a good night, Braxton."

Chapter 9
Braxton

The metal door creaked when I pushed it open. The warehouse we owned held all of our equipment and had a small room we used for practice sessions when off the road. I was the first one to arrive, and while I waited, I spent the time setting up my kit, making sure it was ready for when the rest of my band arrived.

I had to shake the pictures of Abby from my mind. She was angry with me when I dropped her off at her apartment. I didn't walk her in. I didn't even speak a word to her. She was trying her hardest not to cry when she slid out of my truck, slamming the door in protest.

I just couldn't do it. I couldn't be around her. It hurt too much to see her, knowing she was covered in scars. The pain in my chest whenever I thought of her could send me into a bad place. It was a place I spent every moment of my life in since the night I almost killed her. Those scars on her body were mine…all mine.

"Hey man," Ace said as he opened the door, then stopped dead in his tracks. "What's wrong?"

"Nothing," I said, shaking my head. "Nothing at all."

"Bullshit," Ace barked.

"Leave it alone, Ace," I warned.

"I won't leave it alone," he said, narrowing his eyes. "You need to get your shit straight when it comes to Abby, because the news I have to share is going to be huge. I can't have you running off all half-cocked when we leave town again."

"Man, I'm good," I promised, hoping my expression didn't give away how not good I actually was when it came to Abby.

"What news?" Cash asked as he entered. Our bassist set his case against the wall and moved close. Ace just gave me a pointed look and turned around to greet the others.

"Yeah, what's going on?" Taylor asked as he came in with his guitar case.

"Looks like we just booked a three month tour opening for *Bleeding Secrets*," Ace said with a grin. "This is huge."

"Hell yes, it is!" Cash laughed. "They've been all over the charts for months now."

"Their shows bring in a lot of people," Cash mentioned, pulling his long, blond hair up into a ponytail.

"This is going to be good for us," Ace remarked, looking at his phone.

I nodded when necessary, knowing that my vote wasn't needed. Anything that boosted our career was good in my book. There was only one question I needed to know the answer to. "When do we leave?"

"Three weeks." Ace frowned. "Why?"

"Just wondering," I shrugged, hiding my wince. I had hoped we would leave immediately. That way, I could get away from Abby all that much quicker.

We spent the next four hours putting together a set list and practicing. After that, we worked on new songs for our next album. We'd probably go into the studio after the upcoming tour. It was never too early to start making music and planning for the next album release.

Presley and Coraline showed up with pizza, forcing everyone to take a break. Ace and Presley chatted about the song that was to be recorded on her next album. *Witch's Spawn* had been in the studio for the past two days, and Ace was going to sing the new song with her.

I was happy for him and Taylor. Those two deserved so much. After all they'd been through over the past several years, settling down looked good on them.

I refocused my gaze on my kit and adjusted one of my cymbals as I thought about how I could've had that at one time, but I had destroyed it.

By the time we finished, my mood had soured and I just wanted to leave, but the guys were having none of that. As the door to the warehouse opened, I realized my sister wasn't going to get off my back about Abby either, because she'd brought the woman who owned my heart with her.

"Before you growl at me, just know I didn't want to come, but she made me," Abby told me as I approached, hooking a thumb over her shoulder to indicate Penny was behind dragging Abby out of the apartment.

Jesus, she smelled amazing. It took all of my willpower not to tangle my hands in her hair and take her lips with my own. There was a time when I would've done just that. There'd never been a time when I didn't remind her that she was mine. I used to own her love, and I cherished it…until I destroyed it.

The sway of her hips was not forced as she began to walk away. No, Abby never tried to look sexy; it just came naturally. Fuck, I had to stop looking at her like that. It took me a second to get my wits about me, but when I did, I frowned when I noticed she was holding onto her scarred arm.

"What's wrong?" I asked, walking up behind her and placing my hand on her shoulder. When she shrugged me off, I felt my anger boil. If someone had harmed her again, I'd probably kill them for sure this time. "Talk to me."

"No," she said, walking away to take a seat on a lone stool over in the corner.

"You're in pain, aren't you?" I accused as I followed her. She didn't need to confirm it, I could see it in her beautiful eyes.

"Maybe a little," she admitted with a heavy sigh. "I'm okay, Braxton, really. I'm just tired."

"Have you not been sleeping?" I pulled a chair over and turned my body toward her, realizing that was a mistake when my knee brushed hers. Why did one simple touch send a stabbing pain directly to the center of my heart?

"No," she answered, pulling her hair over the left side of her neck to hide the scars from me, and it gutted me.

"I'm sorry," I whispered. "I wish there was something I could do."

"I always have problems sleeping after a surgery, Braxton. It'll be better in a few days. Please, don't cause a scene."

Coraline handed Abby a plate with a slice of pizza. I left her to talk to the girls and grabbed some food for myself. I watched her laugh and smile as she talked to them, and I wished things were different. I'd give anything to go back to the day I almost killed her.

"We will have a break about three weeks into the tour," Ace said as he came up to my side. I didn't miss when his eyes flickered over toward the couch where Abby was sitting. "You can come home."

"I don't know, Ace," I said, rubbing at a pain in the center of my chest. "This is hard."

"She obviously loves you," he replied, dropping his plate into the trash bin behind the table. "Stop running away from her."

"I'm not running." I frowned. "I'm doing what's best for both of us."

"No, you're running, man." He lowered his voice as he moved closer. I was taller than my lead singer, but he had no problem getting into my face. "You'll never be happy until you make things right with that woman."

"You don't understand," I replied, wiping a hand over my face.

"What happened between you two?" he inquired, taking a small step away. "You can tell me."

"Can we not do this here?" I begged, looking over my shoulder. Abby was talking to Coraline and Presley. They were deep in conversation, and I willed her to look up at me, but she didn't.

"We can do it here or outside," he said, narrowing his eyes. "You are not alone in this, Braxton."

I disposed of my trash without another word and started walking toward the back door of our warehouse. Ace wasn't far behind me. I had never told them exactly what had happened with Abby, but I was sure they had some idea. It was no secret in our band that we all had our demons and guilt over things from our pasts.

The sun hit my face as I pushed the door open wide. It was nice to see the sun after several days of dreary weather. The picnic table off to the side of the door was dry enough for me to take a seat on top as Ace took to the actual bench on the other end, giving me enough space.

"I almost killed her," I began, seeing Ace flinch out the corner of my eye. "I was coming off a high, and she saw the marks in my arm as we were driving on the highway. We had a fight and the next thing I knew, I smelled smoke. My body was on the highway, broken so badly I couldn't get to her. She was pinned in the car and it was on fire."

"Fuck," Ace cursed under his breath.

"She's burned down the left side of her body," I continued. "There have been numerous surgeries and treatments over the past three years. I'd avoided her as best as I could, but she finally came to the show last week to confront me."

"Why?" Ace asked.

"Because I've been paying her bills." I shrugged. "It's the only way I can ensure she is taken care of for the things I did."

"She's mad about you paying the bills?" Ace pushed, looking for more answers.

"Yeah," I replied with a harsh curse. "She has insurance, but I made sure that everything she ever needed would be taken care of when I went to jail."

"Are you still paying, Braxton?" he asked, looking down at his feet.

"Of course," I scoffed. "Why would I ever stop paying for her care?"

"Because she isn't yours," he replied, making my hands tighten where I had them wrapped around the edge of the table. "You said so yourself."

"She is mine," I barked, feeling my anger bubble to the surface. I had to take a few deep breaths before I lost my shit and punched the wall behind me. "But I can't be with her."

"What are you going to do when she finds someone who accepts her for who she is now? Scars and all?"

"I'll kill him," I replied, feeling my heart ache.

"That's not fair to her. You need to let her go." Ace stood from his seat and turned to face me. I saw the pain in his eyes. I knew what was coming next, and I begged him with my eyes to not say it out loud, but it was no use. "Or love her the way she deserves to be loved, my friend."

Back inside, I ignored the women and found my place behind my kit. Ace and Taylor were already in place. Cash came in and grabbed his bass. I started playing and forced myself to practice the new song we'd written. I lost myself in the music, and I tried my hardest not to watch Abby from the corner of my eye.

Penny was sitting front and center, her eyes on Cash. I wondered for a moment what that meant, but I didn't think he was my sister's type. She wouldn't date my bandmate anyway, because I'd cut off his pride if he ever touched her. That was a fact he could take to the bank.

After the next song, I saw Penny walk outside with Presley and Abby. Presley held up her hand to Ace, indicating she'd be back shortly. The door closed and we continued to play. It didn't take long before Presley returned alone, and she took a seat next to Coraline. I raised a brow at both women when they looked my way, but all I got was a sad shake of Presley's head as my answer.

Abby had gone home for the night.

Chapter 10
Abby

The air vent didn't make a sound as the cool air blew across my bare skin. The doctor examined my healing arm and his gentle touch was something I'd become acquainted with more than any patient should. I'd been here more times than I could count over the past few years, and he was as close to me as a friend.

"You're healing amazingly, Abagail," Doctor Barnett said, writing something in my chart. "How's the stiffness?"

"Almost gone," I replied, pulling the sleeve of my top back into place.

"Pain?" he continued, looking up at me over the top of his wire-rimmed glasses.

"Occasionally," I admitted.

"I want to see you again in a month." He smiled. "Hopefully, we can stretch out these appointments."

"That would be nice." I sighed and looked down at my feet. "Will I ever be okay?"

"It all depends on how you are healing," he said, slipping his pen into his coat pocket. I plucked quietly at the paper covering over the exam table, not realizing I was making a mess with the tiny pieces. "You will always have visible damage, but my goal here is to make it so you don't have to have too many surgeries to remove the scar tissue at your joints. Your mobility is what concerns me."

"I feel better than before this surgery," I blurted.

"I can tell. You look happier," he observed.

"I have no idea what you're talking about," I teased.

"Yes, you do." He winked. "Go see the man that put that look on your face. I haven't seen you this cheerful in a long time."

I nodded and slid off the table, not commenting on his observation. I wasn't happy, but I wasn't sad either. Braxton had come back into my life, but that didn't mean things would work out between us.

I drove my car over to Penny's apartment. She was cleaning the kitchen when I entered. She waved me over to the table and told me to take a seat while she put away some folded towels from the small laundry room off to my right.

"Okay," she huffed. "I'm ready. Are you sure you are up for this?"

"Yeah," I answered, biting my bottom lip. The band was meeting at Ace and Presley's home for a cookout and some time together before they headed out on tour in two weeks' time. Braxton hadn't put up a fuss when Presley had asked me at the warehouse after their practice.

"Let's go," she said with a smile, grabbing her bag from the back of the chair.

Penny shuffled through the radio stations as I used my GPS to find the address Presley had given me. I smiled when a *Fatal Cross* song came on the radio, feeling a sense of pride for Braxton and all of his accomplishments since getting himself clean. I was happy he had found a home with Ace, Taylor, and Cash. His old band was no longer together and, as far as I knew, they'd all but disappeared.

Lights were on outside the home on a hill as I parked in the driveway. The garage door was open and music could be heard from the backyard. Penny walked ahead of me and entered the home. I hesitated, thinking she was crazy for just walking into their home without knocking. I followed and was relieved when Presley scooped me up into a hug.

"I'm so glad you came," she said, careful of my left side. I was sure Braxton had told them about my injury. I was thankful they were careful, because I was still healing and didn't want to reinjure myself in any way. It sucked having to be so cautious, but over the past few years, I had come to accept that and just kept living my life.

"Thank you for having me."

Presley ushered us out back where everyone was gathered on a wooden deck. My eyes automatically fell on Braxton where he was sitting alone at a table by the steps that led down to the backyard.

"Hey," I said as I approached. My voice sounded soft, but I was breathless. He looked sexy as hell, wearing a short sleeved shirt that wasn't ripped all to hell, a pair of jeans that hugged the muscles in his legs just right, and a pair of aviator sunglasses that made him look deadly.

"Here, take my seat," he said, making a move to stand, but I held my hand out to stop him. "I can take this one. Don't get up."

Braxton nodded and leaned back in his chair. There were a few minutes of awkward silence, and I was about to get up to go find Penny when he finally sat forward. "Can I get you something to drink? We don't have any hard alcohol, but I can go get you a beer if you'd like."

"No, Braxton." I shook my head. "I can't drink on my medicines. A water will be just fine. Thank you." He didn't waste any time in going inside, returning with a bottled water.

"Dinner is almost ready," Ace announced as he lifted the lid on the grill. The smell of hamburgers filled the air, and I giggled when my stomach let out a sound of need.

"You're hungry." Braxton frowned, making a statement as he turned for the grill. He picked up the plate Ace had just filled and took it inside. I followed behind him, because if he was the same man I'd loved all those years ago, he would get grumpy if I didn't eat.

When I entered the kitchen, he was already making a plate. I stood off to the side and waited my turn, but I didn't need to wait long. "Here. I made it the way you like it."

"You remember?" I asked in wonder. How could he remember that after all this time?

"I remember everything about you," he mumbled as he stepped away from the counter to allow Coraline to make her plate. Presley and Penny followed. We all sat in the living room, using the large coffee table as our gathering point. I sat cross-legged on the floor and ignored Braxton's scowl. Penny sat on my left, but I saw her glance up out of the corner of her eye at the long-haired bassist. A slight blush painted her cheeks before she picked up her food and began to eat. I didn't say anything, but I did smile a little. She obviously thought Cash Roberts was good looking.

"Your brother will kill you," I whispered when I realized everyone was involved in other conversations; mostly about music and the upcoming tour.

"I can look," she giggled.

My eyes flicked up toward Cash, and he was staring at Penny over the rim of his glass. I heard Braxton grunt, and when the bassist looked away, I caught Braxton's eye, giving him a hard stare.

Ace's phone rang and he excused himself to answer it. Presley watched him as he paced in the kitchen, talking softly to someone who was obviously important. Coraline turned around to watch him, also.

"What's going on?" Coraline asked as Ace returned.

"Just some scheduling conflicts with media stuff," he hedged, casting a glance at Taylor. I was confused, not knowing much about their business.

"Tell me," Coraline demanded. "I'm still your tour manager, even if I'm going to be stuck behind the fucking merch booth."

"You're still our tour manager," Taylor promised, placing a hand on her stomach. "We just don't want you overdoing anything."

"Stop sugar-coating shit, Taylor," she growled. "I swear you guys are going to drive me crazy. Ace, you better tell me what was said."

"I'm getting an email with what radio stations we will need to visit while on this tour," he paused, "It's a lot, Cora."

"And?" she asked, raising her brow. "I can handle it. Send me the email."

"We need you at the venue to set up merch." Taylor frowned. "You can't do both."

"The hell I can't," she sighed. "We will just hire someone to sell merch while I handle what I'm supposed to handle."

"How are we going to find someone in two weeks?" Cash asked, setting his napkin on his empty plate.

"I don't know of anyone off the top of my head, but I can ask around." Cora tapped her lip with a finger.

"I'll do it," I blurted, causing everyone in the room to turn toward me. I felt like a sculpture on display in a clown factory. "What?"

"No," Braxton answered first. Shaking his head, he looked at all of his band mates and repeated his statement. "No."

"Why not?" I asked, feeling a little put out that he was answering for me. "It can't be that hard. I worked retail for eight years."

"It's not that hard." Coraline rolled her eyes. "I can teach you everything you need to know."

"Are you serious?" I smiled. I'd never even thought about going on tour with Braxton. To be honest, I hadn't even thought about what I said before I'd opened my big mouth, offering my time.

"I'm fine with it," Ace said, looking over at Taylor, who nodded. Cash gave me a little wink before nodding. Braxton was the only one who wouldn't give his approval.

"She cannot do it with her injuries," he finally admitted.

"I can too." I frowned, knowing he was partially right. "I'll be healed from my surgery by the time you head out, Braxton. The only thing I cannot do is lift heavy things."

"The boxes of shirts are too heavy for even Coraline," he stated.

"Those are brought in by the crew anyway," Cora corrected. "You wouldn't have to lift anything."

"I'd like to go." I shrugged, keeping my eyes off of Braxton. I didn't need to look at him to know he was pissed. "I need a job anyway."

"I'll get you set up." Cora clapped. "Yay! More girls! I won't be alone."

Braxton stood up from his seat and stormed out of the room. We all flinched when the back door slammed. Ace started to go after him, but I held my hand out. "Leave him be. He will calm down."

"He's being an asshole," Cash growled.

"He just needs some time to come to terms with this and he will be fine." I smiled, hoping my bottom lip didn't quiver. "Trust me. I'll go speak with him."

Chapter 11
Braxton

I had two weeks left before it was time to roll out. We had so much planning to do and a short amount of time to get it done. Didn't matter to me anyway. I lived for the constant movement. I didn't like staying bored for long, because that caused my mind to wander too far away from what I deemed comfortable.

Coraline overstepping me and inviting Abby to go out on tour with us just pissed me off. She had no business around dirty venues and seedy cities. She was injured, and I didn't have time to watch over her.

The sun had set by the time I stormed out of the house. I just needed a minute to calm down. I heard the sliding door open, and I stiffened when her scent reached me. My body relaxed when her tiny hand touched my shoulder. "Braxton?"

"Abby," I warned, reaching up to remove her hand, but I defied myself by taking her hand into mine as I turned around. My thumb softly rubbed the back of her soft hand. She was so tiny in my eyes and so fragile to the world. "This job isn't for you."

"I beg to differ," she argued. "I can do it, Braxton, and it isn't your call anyway. I'm a grown woman who can make her own decisions. Things are different now."

"I know they are." I frowned, feeling that ton of guilt weigh on my chest.

"Stop that," she barked, causing my eyes to look up from the ground. "This difference isn't about what happened."

"Isn't it?" I asked.

"No," she scoffed. "Jesus, Braxton. You think I'm nothing but a weak female who can't take care of herself. Well, I have been taking care of myself. Ever since you left me in that hospital bed, I have done nothing but fight my way back…and I did it *alone*."

"I couldn't be there, Abby," I reminded her. "I had my own injuries, and then they took me to jail for what I did."

"Why didn't you answer my letters?" she asked, punching me in the heart again.

"I don't want to talk about this here," I told her, proud of myself for not yelling.

"We are going to talk about this here, because I have so much to say." She didn't release my hand when she made the move back to the chairs where we had been sitting earlier. I took a seat and waited until she sat beside me. I thought of several excuses to leave, but none of them would fall from my lips. "Answer my question."

"I tore them up when they were delivered," I replied. Her touch felt electric and reminded me of better times. Times when things were good and normal.

"Why?" Her thumb rubbed circles across the tattoo of a king of hearts on my thumb. It was a tattoo I had gotten last year, because she used to call me her king.

"I didn't want to know how much you hated me," I admitted. Why did remembering all of the good times hurt so bad, and why did bringing up what happened gut me just as badly?

"I never hated you, Braxton," she said, reaching up to touch my face. The contact was like coming home and that scared me senseless. I wasn't supposed to feel that electricity anymore. It'd been too long since I'd felt the love she had for me just through the contact with my skin.

"I hate myself," I replied, shaking my head. "I don't know why we are discussing this, Abby. I'll always feel this way, and being with you will never make it go away."

"I think it's good that I'm going with you on this tour," she said. "Maybe we can find some middle ground and at least be friends again?"

"Okay." I nodded. I didn't know what else to say to her. She obviously was going on tour with us, no matter how much I put up a fuss. I didn't like it, but I was going to have to accept it.

"Thank you, Braxton," she whispered, leaning over and kissing my cheek.

I watched her return to the house, softly sliding the door closed. I sat there for several minutes staring after her, and I refused to wipe away the tear that leaked out of my eye when the pain in my chest was no longer present.

I wanted to push her away, but I didn't want her to let me go, either. She was my world. No matter what lies I told myself, my heart would always belong to Abby.

Always.

Chapter 12
Abby

We were leaving today. I'd packed my bags, careful to keep my stuff to a minimum. I didn't want to step on anyone's toes, but Coraline assured me there was plenty of room for all of my things.

It was raining and a bit chilly. I'd been feeling better over the past week, and I was ready for this adventure. I'd only traveled out of Seattle once, to Hawaii for a summer vacation a few years before I met Braxton. From the look of the schedule I'd seen, we would be seeing almost all of the United States over the next couple of months. I couldn't wait!

"You ready?" Coraline smiled, walking toward the front of the bus. She stopped and unlocked a compartment, pulling the door open wide. "You can put your large suitcase in here and your smaller backpack can go into your bunk."

Coraline had explained to me that I should carry a bag onboard the bus with a few days' worth of clothes and essential needs like my toiletries. I could swap out what I needed whenever we were at a venue. I hefted my bag into the spot she'd said would be my own and let her close the door. She handed me a small brown key to use to access it when I needed.

A large SUV pulled up and the door swung open. Cash and Ace stepped out and walked around the back. They retrieved their belongings and made their way over to the back of the bus to store their bags in a different, larger bin.

"Hey, Abby." Ace smiled as he approached. "Who all are we missing?"

"Braxton." I frowned. "He should've been here by now."

"No worries," Taylor said as he rounded the front of the bus. "He won't be late."

I made myself stay busy by arranging my bunk. It was the second one from the bottom and the easiest to climb in and out of, ensuring I wouldn't put any strain on my arm. There was plenty of room and a light for me to use if I wanted to read late at night. It was cozy and all mine.

I heard his heavy footsteps as he boarded. I turned and looked toward the front of the bus, our eyes locking as soon as he looked up. He didn't say anything, just casted his gaze aside after a few seconds and moved toward where I was standing.

"Are you settled?" he asked, tossing a backpack into the bunk below me.

"Yes, Coraline helped me get my things situated."

"The buses will leave soon. Might as well make yourself comfortable," he suggested as he straightened.

"I think I will lay down while we travel," I said. "I'm trying to change up my days and nights. Coraline said we'd be up at some weird hours."

"Abby," Braxton sighed heavily, "are you sure you want to do this? It isn't the easiest life."

"I am," I replied. "I really want to go. Please, Braxton, don't make this an issue."

"I just worry about you," he admitted, stunning me silent for several seconds while he just stared at me.

"Thank you, but I can take care of myself," I replied, but mentally kicked myself when I saw the flash of guilt cross his face. He started to turn away from me, but I reached out and clamped my hand over his wrist. "I didn't mean that in any way to upset you. I just want you to understand I'm not as fragile as you think I am."

"In my eyes, you are as delicate as the most exotic flower," he said, pulling his arm back and turning on his heel. I let him walk away from me, even though I didn't want him to go. It was going to take a lot of effort to get Braxton to stop this nonsense. I was going to be fine.

"Oh, Braxton," I whispered under my breath.

I climbed into my bunk and closed my eyes, only waking slightly when I felt the bus pull away from the parking lot.

An hour later, I awoke with a nagging pain in my arm. I didn't want to take any pain medicines, but when I tried to stretch my arm, I realized I was going to be miserable without it. I flipped on the small lamp above my head and reached for the small bag I had tucked at my feet. There was a warm bottle of water in the mesh side pouch that ended up being exactly what I needed. I took the pill and pulled the blanket up over my shoulders.

It was only five in the afternoon, and we had another sixteen hours of driving before we arrived in Los Angeles for the first show of the tour. The schedule would have us spending the day in northern California, so our driver would be able to rest. Coraline had mentioned that she wanted to go check out some mall in the area, and I'd agreed to go.

The show was two days away, and I was ready to see *Fatal Cross* perform for the second time in my life. I chuckled to myself as I thought about how ridiculous that sounded. If I was going to be working for them, shouldn't I have better knowledge of their show? Thankfully, I knew their songs, but that was about it.

My eyes fluttered closed, and I reached up to turn off my light. I closed my eyes again, not thinking I would actually fall asleep, but I must have, because I was woken up when Braxton parted my curtain slightly. "We have food. You should eat something."

"I'm not hungry," I mumbled as I burrowed down further into my pillow.

"Abby," he whispered. I felt his hand touch my hip, and I opened my eyes, not realizing how close he actually was. "Please come eat."

"I'd rather sleep," I slurred, seeing Braxton frown.

"Are you hurting?" he asked. "Did you take something?"

"Yeah," I nodded. "Nothing too strong. I think I laid on my arm wrong when I fell asleep. I'll be alright."

"If you're sure," he replied.

"I am," I yawned. "Please, just let me rest."

Braxton didn't say anything else, just let the curtain fall. Darkness took me back into a peaceful sleep.

Chapter 13
Braxton

Fatal Cross hadn't played a venue this large since before I'd come along. The fact that we were opening for *Bleeding Secrets* meant things were looking up for us. It seemed like overnight we'd gone from playing for three thousand fans to almost ten thousand.

Our latest single had only been out for two weeks when Ace had gotten the call. Being direct support for this huge tour could be the door we needed opened to move up to our own headlining spot. We were on the cusp of something huge, and now was the time to work our asses off for that spotlight.

Coraline made her way off the bus, resting a hand on her very small baby bump. I watched as she moved toward the trailer that transported all of our gear. She spoke with Liam and pointed toward two cases. When she started to pick up a box of shirts, he took it from her and shook his head. I laughed when she flipped him off and stormed away. I couldn't contain my smirk as she approached me, looking as pissed off as a wet cat.

"I'm pregnant, not incapable," she growled.

"You're not allowed to lift anything too heavy, you know this," I reminded her. "You're still the tour manager. Just not a roadie."

"Yeah, I know." She frowned. "I miss working."

"It won't be forever," I said. I wasn't sure what their plans were for after the birth of their child. I was sure Taylor would want her to stay home with the kid, but knowing Cora, she'd live on the road and be a mom all at the same time.

"I need to go," she sighed, casting a glance over her shoulder at the men who were pushing cases up to the venue. "Please be on the bus at six for dinner."

"Okay." I nodded and watched her follow our crew inside.

Ace bounded down the stairs of the bus and stopped when he saw me leaning against the side. He looked at his phone and slipped it into his back pocket before copying my pose.

"When does *Witch's Spawn* head out on their tour?" I asked, curious as to how my vocalist was handling being without his new bride.

"Day after tomorrow." He paused, taking a moment to look up at the sky. "I'm not worried, but I'm worried."

"Those boys are not going to let anything happen to her," I said, knowing her band was as close to Presley as any blood bond could ever be. She was going to be fine.

"I know," he said, chewing on his bottom lip.

"Are we going to cross paths with them at any point on this tour?" I pushed.

"A few times." He smiled, running a hand through his curly hair. "We are planning on meeting up in about ten days."

"Good," I said, pushing away from the bus. I was happy for him, but knowing he would be seeing his wife soon put me in a sour mood, knowing I couldn't have Abby. She wasn't mine anymore. "Cora said food would be on the bus at six. I'm going to my bunk for an hour."

"Okay, man," Ace replied, but he was already retrieving his cell phone. I was sure he planned on pestering her until it was time to go on stage.

I slid into my bunk and closed the curtain to block out most of the light. Closing my eyes was necessary. My mind was tired, even though my body was coiled tight with excitement for the tour. The constant highs and lows to this business could drive someone mad.

Her soft giggle woke me from a dreamless sleep. I stared into the darkness for several seconds while I tried to remember the last time that had happened, and frowned when I couldn't. My sleep had been disturbed since the night of the accident, and I didn't know anything else besides Abby's screams as my body lay paralyzed in the bed.

"That's not funny, Liam." Abby giggled again. "You have no shame."

"With a pretty woman like you, I can't help myself," Liam replied. His obvious flirting sent my feet to the floor. I wrenched the door to the bunk room open and marched forward. Our roadie's eyes widened as I approached.

"What the fuck did you say to her?" I demanded, clenching my fists at my sides. I didn't want to punch him, because he was half my size, but I'd do it if he was being less than honorable with her.

"Braxton!" Abby gasped and stepped between us. I didn't want to touch her damaged arm, but I would if I needed to move her out of the way. Why the hell was she defending him anyway? "It was nothing!"

"It better have been nothing," I warned, narrowing my eyes. Liam mumbled out an apology and tucked his tail between his legs, fleeing from the bus.

"How *dare* you be mean to that man," Abby growled as she put her tiny hand on my chest. "We were teasing each other. He wasn't being rude."

"He was flirting with you," I replied, still looking over her shoulder at the empty space left from where Liam had been standing.

"And?" she pushed. "So what if he was?"

My heart roared in my chest. The thought of another man looking at her with lust in his eyes sent me over the edge. I tried to brush past her, but she stood her ground, knowing I wouldn't touch her.

"He's a dead man."

"Oh, shut the hell up, Braxton," she scoffed. "We are not together, and I can flirt with anyone I want."

"You think so?" I snarled, stepping up close. She had to look way up to glare into my eyes. I saw the fire in them that made me love her back then, and in the back of my mind, I knew beyond a shadow of a doubt I still loved her now.

"Yes, actually…I do," she continued as she moved forward so that we touched. I felt her breasts as they came in contact with my chest. I squinted my eyes, praying that her touch wouldn't affect me, but it did. It always did. "I am not yours anymore, Braxton."

"You will always be mine," I whispered as I cupped her face, careful of the scarring on her neck. I pressed my lips to hers, knowing what I was doing was a bad idea, but I needed her touch. Just once more.

As our lips connected, I felt her body relax. She let me devour her lips, taking control like I always did with our love making. Abby was very submissive when it came to my wishes, and she had the power to bring me to my knees so I was the one worshiping her.

I was stunned when her hands came up to squeeze the tops of my shoulders. Her soft tongue swept out and found my own. I slipped my hand into her hair and closed it into a fist, holding her tightly to my lips as if she'd slip from my grasp at any moment.

"Don't let me go, Braxton," she whispered as I started to release my hold and pull away from her embrace. "Please…"

"I won't ever let you go, Abby," I began, sighing heavily as I moved my hand from her hair to the top of her uninjured shoulder. "I cannot seem to get you off of my mind, but when you are around, it's easier to remember what we had."

"What about the nightmares?" she asked, her face falling with the question. I'd yelled at her and told her about hearing her calling for me in my sleep.

"I didn't have one today," I admitted.

"What about yesterday?" she asked, talking a small step away. I felt lost without her close, but I didn't pull her back. I needed room to breathe.

"Yes," I admitted on a growl, feeling uncomfortable talking about them.

"I hate it that you have so much guilt, Braxton," she replied, biting on her bottom lip. I reached up and pulled it from her teeth with my thumb.

"You always do that when you are nervous," I said, dropping my hand.

"I know," she said with a smile. "Habit."

The door to the bus opened and Cash entered the living room as he slipped his phone into his back pocket. He ignored us and moved toward the bunk area, pulling his clothes from his bag. He mumbled something about a shower and disappeared into the small bathroom at the back of the bus.

"I need to get inside to finish setting up the merch booth with Coraline," Abby said, excusing herself. "We will talk later."

"Okay," I replied, taking a seat on the couch as I watched her leave.

Somehow, the pain in my chest was gone. I felt lighter, more like my old self. My mind knew Abby was the cause of it, but I couldn't let go of it all at the snap of my fingers. I'd always have guilt for almost killing her. Every single time I saw the puckered skin of the scars, I'd be reminded of taking something so precious and destroying it.

Chapter 14
Abby

The headlining band, *Bleeding Secrets*, was already inside as we entered the back door. Four very handsome rockstars stood around talking to Ace and Taylor. Braxton came up beside me as I walked. I didn't say anything to him, feeling a little loss at the fact he didn't hold my hand or even really acknowledge I was there. I didn't want to look too deeply into his kiss, either, but I would be lying if I didn't admit I wanted more.

The fact he actually touched me that way was one step I honestly didn't think would happen for us. He'd been so hell bent on not even being in my presence just a few weeks ago. Now, I was on tour with the band and working as part of their crew. The pay was good, but I didn't even need it. I was happy just being around him, because I'd missed him so much. The *old* Braxton was the one I missed, not this newer, sadder version of the man I'd known for five years.

"Hey, Brax," Ace called out, turning from his position to see us walking together. Ace gave me a warm smile and began his introduction.

"Braxton, Abby," he began, holding his hand out toward the other band. "This is Michael Ryan, Jesse Majors, Preston Salvatore, and Archer Moss of *Bleeding Secrets*. Guys, this is my drummer, Braxton Keller, and our merch girl, Abby Hampton."

"Hello," they said, almost in unison.

"Hi." I waved as Braxton shook everyone's hand.

Those men were completely, one hundred percent rockstars, and even though I'd never seen them before, the air of authority and famousness that rolled off of them made me feel a little awkward, but it didn't take long for me to realize they were just like everyone else.

"I heard there's food somewhere." Preston smiled, looking around the backstage area as if he could just summon food to appear. "I'm starving."

"You're always starving." Archer laughed, running a hand through his dark hair. "I think they are catering out to the buses in about twenty minutes."

A very handsome guy with short, black hair approached, and I was momentarily struck silent by his pretty boy looks and stunning blue eyes. His left arm was covered in tattoos and I noticed he acted a little shy, proving my guess by standing by silently until Archer introduced us. He cleared his throat before speaking up. "I'm Jesse Majors. Nice to meet you."

We stood around and mingled for about fifteen more minutes. I found out that Archer Moss was the lead singer for *Bleeding Secrets*, Jesse Majors was their bassist, Michael Ryan was the drummer, and Preston Salvatore played guitar.

Braxton narrowed his eyes at Jesse when he stared at me a little longer than necessary. I wanted so badly to reach out and touch Braxton just to let him know I was only interested in him. Jesse gave Braxton a shrug when he noticed the fire in his eyes and excused himself.

I watched the tall, brown haired bassist walk away. He was really good looking; like a picture perfect cover model with massive amounts of tattoos up and down his arm, just like Braxton.

"If you guys need anything, please let us know," Archer said, shaking our hands again before he left.

"I have to go," Braxton said, turning toward me. "I'll see you after the show."

"Okay." I nodded, hoping he would touch me again, but he just…didn't.

I left him and found my way out to their booth. Liam was there, sitting in a folding chair. He looked up when I approached, but frowned. "Are you okay?"

"I'm good," I shrugged.

"If you're sure," he pushed, looking around me to look for something. He reached for the money box and handed it over. "If you need anything, give me a call."

"I will," I nodded, taking the seat he offered.

I heard Ace belt out the beginning of their first song, and I found myself slipping to the side door just a few feet from the booth. No one was around and I had a few minutes, so I could peek through the crack to watch them.

My eyes immediately fell upon Braxton, and I released a sigh of frustration. He was still going to beat himself up over what had happened. I didn't know what I was going to have to do to change his way of thinking.

The next song began, and I continued to stand there, absorbing every moment I could. The thrill of watching *Fatal Cross* on the stage was not going to go away anytime soon. Seeing them perform was breathtaking, and the fact that they were on a much bigger stage than the last time I saw them just made my heart flutter with excitement.

They were two songs from the end of their set, and I was already in place to handle sales after the show. Coraline said I would probably have some people come by periodically throughout the show, but to hang on tight after the last band played because it would get hectic.

Several people hovered over by the bathrooms, looking over the shirts that were displayed over my head. It wasn't until the lights went up in the building that the fans found their way to our table. Liam rushed over when things got crazy, and I found myself smiling at their increasing popularity.

I was really proud of all of them.

Chapter 15
Braxton

I was exhausted. It didn't matter how much I prepared myself, I always ended up sore and tired as soon as the lights went down after our first few shows. I didn't care how tired I was, because this was my life and I loved every moment of it. The blood and sweat was just part of the job.

"Fuck," I groaned as I flopped down on the black leather couch in our green room. This was only the second night of the tour and I already needed a break. The cold air from the vent above gave me goosebumps when it made contact with my sweaty skin. I didn't care, because it felt amazing.

The door opened about fifteen minutes later, and I didn't need to look to see who it was, because I could feel her presence in the room. I pinched the bridge of my nose and took a deep breath, waiting for her to speak first, but she didn't say anything. When I opened my eyes and looked to my left, Abby was quietly looking through her backpack. She didn't look up or speak, and that made me frown.

"What's wrong?"

"Nothing," she mumbled, digging her hand deeper into the bag. I heard the pill bottles inside rattle and my worst fears sent a pain through my chest. "Are you hurting? You need to take it easy, Abby."

"Stop, Braxton," she sighed, pulling a charging cable from the confines of her bag. "I'm okay. I just need to charge my phone, because I want to take some pictures."

"Oh," I said, slumping back into my spot. "Sorry."

"Are *you* okay?" she asked, walking up to my side. I didn't answer her for several seconds, just let my body relax further into the couch. "Braxton?"

"Yeah," I replied, sitting up to stretch. "Just wore out."

"Go rest," she urged, turning for the door. "I'll be out after we finish."

The headlining band was onstage, and Abby would be out front selling our merchandise for at least another two hours. I wanted to reach for her, maybe place a kiss on her lips, but I didn't. I just let her walk out the door.

I had to keep reminding myself that I couldn't have her. Kissing Abby on that bus had been a bad decision. A decision I made when my guard was down. Nothing good would come from us reconnecting, because I'd always be reminded of the accident.

"Hey man," Cash said as he pushed the door open. "Abby said you were in here. I need to ask you something."

"Sure." I cleared my throat and tried to not think about her. It didn't work. "What's going on?"

"I have an idea for a song." He paused, looking at his phone with a frown. "I wanted to go over this with you."

Cash took a seat next to me and handed over his phone. The lyrics were deep and could take on a lot of meanings, but I saw where he was going with his idea. I nodded and handed him back the phone. "I'll work on something."

"Are you okay with that?" he asked, biting his bottom lip.

"Yeah." I nodded, feeling a pain in my chest. His song was more or less about my sister, Penny, and the struggles she'd faced for years. I didn't want to look too much into his lyrics, but I knew that he'd been looking at my sister a little differently since we'd been home. Cash was a manwhore, and I didn't want him fucking around with her, but Penny was a good judge of character and wouldn't let him take advantage of her.

Also, if he fucked over my sister, I'd kill him.

"Alright man," he sighed, "I'm heading to take a shower."

"I'll be out to the bus after *Bleeding Secrets* gets done," I replied, climbing to my feet.

Abby was out at the front of the building, but I couldn't go out there to her. There were thousands of people between us, and I would need a security guard to make it there in one piece. Plus, now that we were playing in small arenas, it wasn't advisable for us to be roaming around without an escort.

Our popularity was climbing faster day by day. It wouldn't be long before we would need our own set of security guards and a bigger crew. The thought of that worried me, but it also thrilled me. This was what the band had worked for since day one. When I came along, Ace, Taylor, and Cash had explained to me that that was their end game...to be number one.

And I had agreed.

The roar of the crowd and the wail of Preston's guitar signaled they were halfway through their set. I found my way out to the side of the stage and watched them. The smoke and lights excited the crowd. Bodies were packed on the floor, and up on the second floor, people were on their feet. There were doors at the back of the venue that were closed. On the other side was a huge area set up for all the bands' merchandise, and that was where my Abby was working.

The building made a huge circle, and I left the side of the stage to see if I could find the door that led to the front where she was. I just needed to lay eyes on her to make sure she was okay. A few of the crew members from *Bleeding Secrets* mingled around, waiting for the show to be over so they could break everything down and load up to head out to our next stop in Phoenix, Arizona.

I came to the end of the hallway and was faced with two gray doors. I carefully pushed on the bar, only opening it a hair so I could see what was on the other side. I smiled to myself when I realized I had found what I was looking for. I didn't have to open it far, because our booth was only about ten feet away, and Abby was standing there talking to Kevin, one of our other roadies. She must've seen the door crack open, because she turned to look in my direction. The corner of her lip lifted in a mischievous smile as she walked over, placing her hand on the door.

"What are you doing?" she growled. "You can't be out here."

"I wanted to check on you," I replied.

"I'm fine," she promised.

"It's about to get hectic out here," I warned. "Are you ready?"

"Yes, Braxton," she giggled. "Get out of here."

"Fine, but call me if you need me," I ordered, hoping she'd listen to me for once.

"I will." Abby rolled her eyes and patted the door. "Go! Before someone sees you."

Nodding, I stepped away from the door and let it close, shutting her out and leaving me to stand there all alone. My heart told me to stay there and take a seat by the door so I could be at her side if she needed help, but my mind screamed at me to give her space.

Abby had changed so much since before the accident. The Abby I knew was soft and submissive. This Abby was strong and independent. I didn't know what to think about her change. It was going to take me some time to get used to seeing her for who she was and not the scarred woman I left in a coma all those years ago.

Chapter 16
Abby

Holy shit! How many shirts did one person want from *Fatal Cross*? The woman who just walked away bought every style they had in stock. I shook my head and helped the next person in line. Kevin and Liam were right next to me, helping out with the crowd. There had to be a hundred people waiting to pick up their souvenirs. I couldn't complain, because the booth for *Bleeding Secrets* had three times the amount of people in line, but they had six people selling the merchandise.

It took about an hour after the show ended to clear everyone out. Placing the back of my hand over my mouth, I covered a deep yawn. Coraline wasn't kidding when she had said it would be crazy. I honestly didn't know how she'd done this ever since she had gotten out of high school.

"You doing okay?" Liam asked, coming up to my side.

"Yeah," I laughed. "I don't think I prepared myself for this."

"Good thing we have about twenty hours before we do it again," he teased, putting a stack of remaining shirts into a box. "We will have a day off on Monday."

Today was Friday, and we had to be in Phoenix tomorrow night for the next show. I shook my head and handed him another stack of shirts. "I will probably sleep until we get to Phoenix, then."

"That's what I do," he chuckled. "Come on. Let's finish up and head to the bus."

It took us another fifteen minutes to load up and get Kevin to load all of the boxes into the trailer. By the time I climbed the stairs to the bus, I was exhausted. I just wanted to take a shower and climb into my bunk.

"How did it go?" Coraline asked as I entered the living room area at the front of the bus. She was sitting crossed-legged on the black leather sofa. Taylor was beside her, but he was busy picking away softly on an acoustic guitar. He looked up and nodded at me, but didn't say anything as he returned playing.

"I'm beat," I yawned. "I think I'm going to shower and crash."

"Good plan," she agreed. "We don't leave for another hour and a half. So, you have time."

I didn't want to ask where Braxton was, and it concerned me that he wasn't in his bunk when

I grabbed my backpack out of my own. His curtain was open and his small bed was made. It didn't look like he'd even laid down since I had seen him peek through the backstage door earlier.

When I walked into the back door of the arena, I looked to my left and decided to stop by the green room to see if he was still there, but didn't find him. Frowning, I made my way over to the showers and hurried through my routine, twisting my hair up in a blue towel to keep it off my shoulders.

I stared in the mirror above the sink and took a long look at my scars. They were there, always staring back at me. I didn't hate them…I didn't love them, either. Those marks were a part of my life, and would be forever. I would live with them…I would die with them. The only thing I regretted about them was Braxton would always look at me and remember what had happened.

I wished I could take those memories from him. He didn't need that guilt in his life, because he was well on his way to the top of the music industry. I wanted the best for him.

Tears fell over my lashes as the pain of realizing I was the one thing that held him back.

If I was being honest with myself, I knew I shouldn't be here. I should've never come on this tour. He needed to move on, as well. Just like he was hoping I would do after all this time.

Pressing my back to the wall, I let my legs give out as I slid down to my butt, not caring about the nastiness of the floor as I held the towel around my body tighter. The longer I kept my eyes closed, the more I saw his face in my mind.

The pain…the anger…the guilt…and my scars.

"What have I done?" I whispered, knowing I was alone.

But I wasn't.

"*Abby?*" Braxton gasped as he stood in the doorway to the women's showers. His large body took up the entire entrance. I wiped my eyes, trying to hide the waterworks. I really didn't want him to see me break down, but as he scooped me up in his arms, I knew my breakdown was going to make things worse. "Are you hurt? Talk to me."

"What are you doing in here?" I sniffled, trying to clear my throat.

"Looking for you," he answered as he walked over to a small bench by the showers. "Damn it, Abby. Tell me what's wrong!"

"I'm fine." Then I panicked, realizing a lot of my scars were visible. "Please, let me get dressed, Braxton."

"Not until you tell me what the fuck happened to you," he snarled. "Did someone come in here? Did they touch you?"

"No, please," I begged, pulling the towel tighter around my body. "Let me put on some clothes, I don't want you to see me like this."

My statement made him freeze, sending his gaze away from my own. I wanted to touch the side of his face and bring it back to mine, but I didn't. It was important that I kept my modesty around him. This would never work out with him. I just couldn't let him see the healed damage of what he'd done.

Thankfully, he carefully set me aside and turned away, placing his face into his hands. "Get dressed," he ordered, but I heard his voice crack at the end.

I scooped up my clothes and locked myself in a stall, pulling on my panties and bra as quickly as possible. My pajama pants were covered in tiny pink and red hearts, and I threw on a red, long sleeved top to sleep in for the night. When I walked out, Braxton was still sitting there, but his head was leaned back against the wall.

"Do you not want me to see the scars?" His question came out as a whisper, and I almost asked him to repeat himself, but I didn't.

"Braxton," I said, taking a seat next to him on the bench. "I didn't think about how hard it would be on you to see me day to day on this tour. I guess when I got out of the shower and looked at myself, I realized what I was putting you through by seeing me. It broke my heart, because I don't want you to feel guilty anymore, but I honestly don't know how to make you understand that I don't hate you, or even blame you, for what happened."

"I don't think I will ever forgive myself," he began. I had to bite the inside of my cheek to keep from crying at his confession. "You were my world, Abby. I'd made a promise to myself to keep you safe from the first day I realized you were mine. That night…that night was me at my lowest point. The drugs were all I wanted, and I couldn't fight the need. When you tried to touch my arm where I'd been injecting the poison, I lost my mind. To realize you touched that, well, it shattered my heart. Then the next thing I knew, I was waking up with two broken legs and the smell of burning metal. I could hear you screaming, calling for me. I was helpless, and I failed my promise to you."

"It was my fault, too," I admitted, holding up my hand when he tried to interrupt me. "Wait, I'm not done."

"Do we really have to talk about this, Abby?"

"Yes," I nodded. "It's time, Braxton."

"Go ahead," he said, defeated.

"I never blamed you," I said, reaching for his hand. He took it without hesitation. "I should've never argued with you in that car. I knew you'd been doing drugs, because you didn't hide it well at all. The night you picked me up, I should've insisted on driving, but I didn't because I didn't want to go against your wishes. I was young and dumb."

Braxton didn't speak for the longest time. I waited, but he just opened and closed his mouth several times. It was obvious he couldn't find the words to explain his feelings.

"I've changed a lot, but I'm still the Abby you knew all those years ago. I've just grown up and had to learn to do things on my own."

"I couldn't be around you," he admitted.

"I understand." I frowned. "I'm sorry."

"What the hell do you have to be sorry for?"

"Being here," I answered, hoping to keep the tears from reappearing. "I know it has to be hard on you, and if it is, I need you to tell me. I will go home and give you peace."

"I don't want you to leave," he replied, his shoulders slumping.

"If it hurts too much…" I began, but let my words trail off.

"It doesn't hurt as bad as I thought it would," he replied.

"I still love you, Braxton," I admitted, wiping away a stray tear, "but I'll leave if it's what you need."

"I need you here," he answered, turning to capture my lips in a gentle kiss.

Chapter 17
Braxton

Lights lit up the stage as the last song began. Ace stood on the riser and belted out the lyrics as I got lost in the music. The crowd roared and swayed along to the music. Taylor played with his head thrown back, and Cash flirted with the women in the crowd.

I couldn't think about the last week of shows. I barely saw Abby, and it put me in the worst fucking mood. I didn't talk to anyone, just did my job and crashed in my bunk as soon as I could. Maybe I was hiding from her, maybe I was just fucking tired from the five days' worth of back-to-back performances.

The lights went down on the stage, signaling our set was over. I wiped the sweat out of my eyes, realizing that I must've played without even realizing it, because I was too busy thinking about Abby.

Our crew rushed past me to take down our set, and I found my way to the green room to lay down on the couch and grab some water. My hands ached from the hell I'd put them through for the past hour.

I heard a commotion outside the door, but didn't make a move to check it out. *Bleeding Secrets* had a ton of security and crew. I was sure whatever that was would be taken care of before things got out of hand.

"Son of a bitch," Ace cursed as he came through the door.

"What the hell was that all about?" I mumbled, not removing my arm from over my eyes.

"Fans," he answered, looking annoyed. "Three guys somehow got backstage and rushed Archer and Preston."

"Fuck," I growled, swinging my legs around so I could sit up. "They okay?"

"Yeah," Ace said, shaking his head. "Their security caught them before things got crazy."

I nodded and fell back against the couch. I was exhausted. I couldn't wait to get to Dallas and spend some time away from all of the craziness of the shows. As much as I loved performing, sometimes I just needed some downtime.

The door to the green room opened and Abby came in, looking around the room. She walked toward a box and squatted down beside it, pulling it open to dig inside.

"Abby?" I called out, startling her.

"Shit, you scared me." She paused, frowning as she got a good look at me. "Are you okay? You look pale."

"I'm exhausted," I answered honestly. "What are you looking for?"

"Ahh, those little button things," she shrugged. "We are out of them."

"Let me help you," I groaned as I rolled off the couch, but didn't make it very far before she was in front of me, pushing me back down onto the couch.

"No, sir," she ordered, shaking her head. "Where's your water?"

"Haven't gotten any yet." I sighed. "Abby, let me help you."

She ignored me and walked over to the fridge in the corner, pulling the door open. She retrieved three bottles and brought them over, handing me two and cracking one open for herself. "Drink."

"Yes, ma'am." I nodded, doing as I was instructed.

I dropped the empty to the ground and opened another one, downing it as quickly as I could. Abby stood there watching me until I was done. She offered me the half bottle she had left, but I waved her off. "No, I'm good. Thank you."

She nodded and returned to the box. I tried not to watch her as she crouched down, but the position she was in made her jeans hug her hips in a seductive way that had my cock hardening in my pants. I licked my lips and started to stand, but mentally kicked myself. I couldn't touch her.

I watched as she grabbed what she had been looking for and left the room. Ace was across the room, watching my every move. He shook his head sadly and grabbed his phone. I didn't say anything to him, just let myself melt back into the couch.

I'd rest and deal with my feelings toward Abby later. Right now, I just needed to cool down and calm my raging erection.

Chapter 18
Abby

Dallas was the place we had three days off, and I planned on getting some laundry done at a local laundromat with Coraline and Taylor after I slept half the day away. Braxton hadn't spoken to me much since the night he found me crying in the showers.

I'd been too busy with running their sales booth at the shows to really be around him, anyway. By the time the last person was out, he was already in his bunk fast asleep. I spent more time helping load up than required, but I was feeling good and I had no pain in my arm. So, I wasn't going to slack on the job I was being paid to do.

I heard Coraline jump out of her bunk and curse. I stuck my head out to see her going into the small bathroom. The pregnancy was hard on her, and I hated to see her sick, but she was stubborn and kept up with everything she needed to do for the band. I honestly didn't know how she did it night after night.

I grabbed my book and slid out of my bunk, pausing as I looked at the drawn curtain to Braxton's bunk. I could hear him breathing softly, and I sighed when I remembered all those times I used to wake up early just to watch him sleep. It'd been so long that I thought I'd forgotten, but obviously, I hadn't.

"Good morning." Ace smiled as I walked toward the coffee pot on the counter.

"Morning," I mumbled and set about making my cup. I took a seat in the dinette across from Ace and looked out the window. We were parked in a hotel parking lot and the sun was shining brightly. I looked at my phone and frowned when I realized I'd slept longer than I'd wanted. It was close to noon, and I needed to make plans for the day.

"I need to find a place to wash my clothes," I mumbled, not really speaking to Ace.

"We are going to stay at this hotel for a few nights," he said. "They have a laundry room you can use so you and Cora don't have to go into town."

"Oh." I frowned, noticing the lead singer had a concerned look on his face. "What's wrong?"

"I'll talk to everyone when they are awake," he promised, holding up his hand. "It's not bad, but I just don't want to repeat myself. Check in time is at four. Take it easy until then."

He stood up and walked toward the bunk area, lifting his phone up to his ear. I heard him greet his wife and then close the partition leading to the back. Wrapping my hands around the mug, I looked down at my left hand when the light hit it just right. My automatic reaction was to hide my scarring, but I quickly realized I didn't need to here.

In fact, ever since I had met the band and their crew, no one had even looked at me differently. I was treated just like a normal human being, and that was refreshing. It felt good to be normal again.

My only concern was Braxton and the fact that he wouldn't even look at the left side of my body. I knew he had a hard time, but I wanted him to look at me the way everyone else in the band did.

"I'm not a freak," I whispered, lifting the cup of coffee to my lips.

The door to the bunks slid open and my heart galloped in my chest. Braxton was walking out in nothing but a pair of black basketball shorts. His hair was tousled and his eyes weren't quite open.

"Morning." I smiled, watching as he made his coffee.

"Morning," he replied, turning from the counter. He stared at me for several seconds before taking a seat on the couch. "What time can we check into the rooms?"

"Um, Ace said around four."

"Okay," he replied, taking another sip of his coffee.

I waited a moment to see if he'd say anything else, and when he didn't, I opened my book and found where I'd left off the night before. Ace returned later, sitting down with everyone to go over some interview dates they had planned for the coming week. It didn't concern me, but I was glad they felt like I was part of the team by keeping me informed of everything. It made me feel more at home with them than before. I was starting to feel like I truly belonged.

"I have another concern," he said, leaning forward. He placed his elbows on the tops of his knees and covered his face for a few seconds before blowing out a deep breath.

"What's going on?" Coraline asked, making a move to be closer to him.

"After talking to *Bleeding Secrets* and their security," he began, taking a second to look at everyone. "I've decided to hire on two security guards to tour with us."

"Is this because of the breach?" I asked, feeling my heart drop into my stomach. The three men were not just fans who were looking to meet their favorite musicians, they had been there for Preston. I wasn't privy to exactly what had happened, but we'd been warned to keep an eye out for anyone who didn't have proper clearance to be backstage from now on.

"Yes," Ace nodded. "I think it would just help us all to have an extra set of eyes around the crew."

The men looked up at Coraline, and then over to me. I didn't care either way what they wanted to do. This was their band, and if hiring extra help was needed, I was okay with whatever they wanted to do.

"That's good," Coraline nodded. "My cousin's band has a whole slew of security that travel with them."

"Abby?" Braxton spoke up after clearing his throat.

"Uh, yeah," I answered. "Sure."

"They'll be here tomorrow," Ace said, standing up from his seat. "Let me know if you have any problems with them. We want to make sure they are a good fit."

Everyone agreed and went their separate ways. Braxton and I were left sitting on the couches, facing each other. We didn't speak for several minutes. He just sat there watching me. I finally couldn't take anymore. "What's on your mind?"

"Your safety," he grounded out through clenched teeth.

"Mine?" I gasped. "I'm perfectly fine. I'm hardly ever backstage anyway."

"But you are alone a lot of times, too," he reminded me.

"Liam is really good about hanging around," I explained, hoping that would put him at ease. I rose to my feet and stretched lazily. "I should get my stuff so I can start my laundry."

"We still have time," he replied, looking at the clock mounted above the dinette.

"What are you going to do for the next few days?" I asked, hoping to get him to talk to me.

"Research this security company." He shrugged. "Sleep and workout some. I've been out of the gym too long."

"I'd like to go with you," I blurted, pausing when I noticed he was looking at my left hand. I closed my fist and put my arm behind my back. When I did, Braxton looked up into my eyes and I saw a fire there I hadn't seen in years.

"Are you up for that?" he asked, standing to his full height. Jesus, he was huge.

"I'm up for anything," I teased, knowing I shouldn't, but the look he was giving me caused a wetness to pool between my legs. Shifting slightly from foot to foot, I tried to calm the ache, but it was useless. I wanted him to touch me so badly.

* * *

I didn't know how we ended up in this hotel room, but my back hit the door as Braxton held my jaw in place, capturing my lips. I felt him all over my body as he took control. I didn't move as he slid the card into the lock and pushed the door open. His hands wrapped around my ass only seconds before he lifted me off of my feet. Wetness surged between my legs, and I tightened my hold around his shoulders as he walked forward. I heard the door close, but I didn't know if he kicked it or it shut on its own…and I didn't care.

I could smell his unique scent of power and alpha male. It was a scent I would remember for the rest of my life. The last thing I wanted to do was get emotional, but as he held me tenderly with his large hands, I felt the stirrings of tears pricking the back of my eyelids. God, I had missed him so much.

His lips pressed against the space just under my earlobe, and I felt a chill roll up my spine. Braxton didn't speak as he removed my cotton shirt, only pulling away to toss it somewhere on the floor. His knees bumped against the bed, and the next thing I knew, I was being laid out like an offering and my jeans were being unbuttoned.

"Braxton," I began, but he quieted me with his signature grunt, telling me to be quiet. He was a beast on and off the stage, as well as in and out of the bedroom.

The inside of my thighs shook as he placed the back of his hand at my knee and slowly made his way to my center. My panties were still on and I rolled my head back when he traced the center with the back of his knuckle.

I wanted to beg him to take them off and touch me, but I didn't. I wanted him to take control, and he did. I heard his belt come free and clang as his pants fell to the ground. When I looked up, he was standing over me, his thick cock grasped in his tattooed hand.

"Take them off, Abby," he ordered, sending my hips in the air as I hooked my fingers into the waistband. I shimmied them down my legs, and I had to bend slightly to push them off to the floor.

I was left there, bare to him in nothing but my bra, but he quickly leaned over to pull my breasts up and over the cups, leaving them on display for his taking. As his tongue laid a path over one nipple, I let out a soft moan. Braxton still didn't speak as he kissed softly across my chest, making his way over to the other one and giving it the same amount of attention.

The bed dipped when he placed his knee between my legs, using the other to nudge them farther apart. I knew how he liked to hold my hands hostage as he gave me pleasure, so I raised them above my head, hiding a wince when I felt a slight pull at my scarred elbow. I wouldn't show any distress with him, because if I even looked like I was in pain, he would stop and leave me alone in this hotel room.

The last thing I wanted was for Braxton to be reminded of that night. He needed to move on, and even if what we were doing was the worst idea in the world, I was going to let him make love to me. It might be wrong, but it was what needed to happen.

It proved to me that he still loved me.

Braxton hesitated for a few seconds, looking into my eyes, before he leaned over me and held my hands with one of his own. My hands were so tiny compared to his. As soon as the contact was made, I tilted my head back and waited for him to capture my lips, and that was exactly what he did.

He was relentless in his lovemaking. His left hand slid down my right side to grasp the back of my thigh, pulling it over his hip. I mimicked the other side and waited for him to either touch me or enter me. I never knew what he would do, and the anticipation had tremors rolling through my legs.

I bit my lip when I almost called out for him to touch me, but he knew what I needed. His fingers traced my lips again, this time with no barriers. I sucked in air through my teeth when he pressed one inside, pausing to allow me to adjust. Within seconds, he added another and then he began to move. His thumb stroked my clit and I felt the stirrings of an orgasm I'd held back for over three years.

"Please," I whimpered, clamping my mouth shut when his eyes narrowed.

"Hmm," he smirked. "You never could keep your pleasure from me."

I knew he was teasing. Braxton liked the control of keeping me quiet until I couldn't handle it anymore. He'd taught me that long ago, promising that it would make my orgasms more intense, and he had been right. I liked the little bit of kink we'd experimented with in the past, and what I'd experienced with him was mind-blowing.

"Tell me if I hurt you," he ordered as he guided his cock toward my body.

"You won't," I assured him, wiggling my fingers to let him know I needed to move. Once he released me, I wrapped my arms around his wide shoulders and pulled him toward my lips. As soon as I kissed him, I felt his cock enter me.

"Fuck, Abby," he growled, moving his hips to a rhythm only he knew would send me over the edge, but I didn't want it to end so soon. I needed more.

His warm chest pressed against mine as he rutted into my core, rolling his hips to ensure he hit the spot that drove me mad. I sounded like a tramp as he increased his speed, urging me over the edge of oblivion.

"Come for me, Abby girl," he whispered in my ear as he buried his face in my neck, grunting with each thrust. I knew he was close, but Braxton would hold off for me. He'd never found his completion without me finding my own before him.

"More, please, Braxton," I begged, holding him tighter to my chest.

Despite my pleas, he used his free hand to slide between us so he could press his thumb to my clit. The pressure, combined with a slow circular motion, sent me over the edge. I called out his name, giving him the clue that I was on the brink of release. My body seized as I closed my eyes tight.

Braxton thrust hard into me, his grunts of pleasure were music to my ears, knowing he was finding his own release in combination with mine. I could feel him pulsing into me, marking me with his seed.

Within a few seconds, he was still, situating himself so he could cup my face with both of his hands. The tender kiss against my lips felt more like a goodbye than a proclamation of his feelings toward me. The moment I felt a tear fall against my cheek, I knew it wasn't from my own eyes…it had come from his.

Chapter 19
Braxton

I still loved her.

I would always love her.

Being inside her again was heaven and hell all wrapped into one. I'd fought it for so long that once I touched her again, all of the anger fled. The guilt was still sitting at the forefront of my mind. There was never going to be a time that I wouldn't look at her and not remember what had happened that day three years ago.

"Braxton," she mumbled as she rolled toward me in her sleep.

"Shh," I whispered, stroking her soft cheek.

I locked down my emotions when my mind started to wander, reminding me that I wasn't what she needed. How could I be? I was a traveling musician. I'd never be home with her. What if we did push this further? How could I let her go through a pregnancy without me? She wasn't like Coraline who had this life in her blood. No, Abby Hampton was too innocent for my lifestyle.

We were total opposites.

"What's wrong?" she asked, sleep clogging her voice. I looked into her eyes and saw the moment she knew I was going to walk out on her. "Braxton, please don't do this."

"I'm no good for you," I said.

"You are everything to me, but I understand if you can't do this," she said. "Just get your things and go, Braxton."

She wasn't crying. Abby just sat up in the bed and used the sheet to cover her breasts. I saw the silvery scars on her arms and looked away quickly.

"I'm sorry," I said as I got out of the bed and picked up my jeans from the floor. I heard the sheets rustle slightly, and when I looked over, she'd rolled over onto her side and faced away from me.

I didn't waste time as I fled from the room, avoiding the elevator. Down at the end of the hallway, I found the stairs and took them two at a time down the seven flights until I came to the bottom floor. It was early morning when I pushed the door open wide and marched outside. The bus was parked at the back of the lot, and that was my destination. I entered the code to unlock the door and went inside, finding no one in the living room.

I needed to wash the scent of her arousal off of me. The last thing I wanted was to wake up with a reminder of the line I'd just crossed. *Fuck! What have I done?*

The water in the small shower was hot, and I made quick work of lathering my body and shampooing my hair. After I let the water rinse all of that away, I closed off the taps and climbed out, wrapping a towel around my waist as I walked out.

"So, this is how it's going to be?" Abby barked from behind me. I gasped and spun around, shocked to see her standing there. Her hair was still in disarray and her lips were swollen from my assault on them.

"Go back to your room, Abby," I growled, turning away from her to search for some clean clothes in my bunk. When I found none, I yanked out a pair of basketball shorts and a tank top that were somewhat clean. I really needed to do some fucking laundry.

"No, Braxton," she continued. "You can't just fuck me and walk out the door the next morning."

"Yes, I can," I replied, slipping my shirt over my head. I didn't warn her before dropping my towel. I noticed how her eyes zeroed in on my erection, proving that I wanted her again. My damn cock had a mind of its own around her.

"You're an asshole," she huffed, turning on her heel and storming from the bus.

That was what I needed to hear from her. Abby shouldn't put me on a fucking pedestal like a goddamned saint. I was better off being labeled as the devil's sidekick for all the things I'd done in my life.

* * *

Ace called us all out to the bus the next morning. Our new security guards were there, and I immediately liked them. Both wore suitcoats and slacks. Neither one of them wore a tie, but their polo shirts were pressed so much, there wasn't a wrinkle in sight.

"This is Hayden Lewis and Marshall Harris," Ace informed us as the men stood at attention in front of us as we waited to shake their hands. After our introductions, the band and crew took seats in various places on the bus. Abby was sitting on the couch, so I took the spot next to her and tried not to curse when she scooted away from me.

Hayden was my size and had the look of a MMA fighter. He couldn't have been older than thirty, and I saw no wedding ring on his finger. From the scar over his eye, I was sure he'd been in a few scuffles in his life. He kept his dark brown hair to military standards, but sported a short beard.

Marshall was slightly younger, and his black hair was long enough to touch the top of his shoulders. He had a pair of aviator sunglasses on that hid his eyes from my view. He wasn't quite as big as Hayden, but he was still built like a goddamn tank.

No one was going to get through those two, and I relaxed knowing Abby would have someone else around to keep her protected when I couldn't be there for her.

"We would like to sit down with everyone and go over a security plan," Hayden announced as he held up a manila folder.

"We would like to keep you guys away from the public during the rest of this tour," Marshall continued. "If you are to go to a radio station for an interview, an appearance where you will be in front of fans, or even an outing for dinner, Hayden and I will be with you."

"What about the crew?" Taylor asked.

"Our main concern is the band itself," Hayden spoke up. I saw the moment when Taylor realized Coraline would be unprotected. I reached out and placed my hand on his wrist to calm him, but it didn't work.

"My wife is part of this crew," he snarled. "And if you haven't noticed, she's pregnant."

"I will not be regulated as to where I can or cannot go," Coraline argued, crossing her arms over her chest.

"I think the entire crew will need to be aware of their surroundings," Marshall interrupted. "We will be able to provide the proper security, but we will need your help by making sure everyone is watching what's going on around them. The incident with *Bleeding Secrets* is more common with bands than you realize. *Fatal Cross* has skyrocketed into the public eye, and you all will need to change your way of thinking about safety."

"We understand," Ace replied, standing from his seat. "We have two female employees, and they are very special to us. Their safety, along with the males on our crew, is extremely important. Would it benefit us to hire on another person to work with you?"

Everyone was on edge. The two men who were sent by the security company Coraline suggested didn't look as if they were worried, and I wanted to trust them, but when we were at a show, the band and crew were so separated most of the time there was no way they could watch over everyone.

After we all agreed to have the company send another person, Hayden and Marshall worked out a plan for us. Abby sat beside me and hung on every word. The thought of someone rushing one of us was scary. The thought of a crazed fan attacking Abby at the merch booth was just another fear that made my blood run cold.

"I won't let anything happen to her," Liam said as he approached me after everyone left the bus to do whatever it was that they were going to do for the rest of the day. My eyes were still on her through the window as she stopped to talk to Cash. I saw him glance up at the window, but he schooled his features and gave her a nod.

"I don't want her out there alone at all," I growled. "She should have someone with her at all times."

"That can be done," Liam agreed.

"I mean it, Liam," I reiterated one last time before turning toward my bunk while everyone else went to their rooms. I would keep to my exile on the bus, because it was safer for me here. I didn't need to be around her unless it was necessary.

Chapter 20
Abby

Two weeks had passed and Braxton was still avoiding me. My mother said she'd buy me a plane ticket to come home, but Penny encouraged me to stay. I was torn. I didn't know what to do.

A new guy, Lane Mathews, showed up the day of the show in Dallas, and introduced himself as the guy who'd be following me around. I didn't like it, but I'd do it for the sake of safety, and the fact that Ace had been so nice about the entire thing. He'd explained to me that there had been some incidents with other bands in the past and people had been hurt. I didn't want anyone to be attacked by crazed fans. So, I nodded and accepted my new bodyguard.

"Your brother is so fucking stubborn," I growled into the phone. We were currently in Kansas City. Taylor and Coraline were away visiting his family with Marshall as an escort, and Cash was on the bus doing business. Braxton disappeared as soon as the wheels on the bus came to a stop behind the arena. Just as he'd done at every show after our romp in the hotel room. Days off were hell, because I didn't know where he was, and I'd be lying if I said I wasn't worried about what he was doing. I was honestly scared he'd relapse, and I prayed I was wrong.

"As much as I hate to say this," she began, "and for the record, it totally grosses me out to say this, but you really need to just seduce him, Abby."

"*What*?" I gasped, pacing the length of the bus. "Have you lost your mind?"

"No," she snickered. "I just know my brother."

"That makes him sound like a manwhore, Penny." I frowned.

"You know what I mean," she tsked. "Wear something tight and sexy, do your hair."

"I can't do that," I scoffed. "I'm not like that."

"Have you ever seen *Grease*?" she laughed.

"No, I'm not doing that," I replied, heat rising to my cheeks. How embarrassing? I couldn't just change who I was to seduce him back into my bed. Hell no!

"Do it, Abby," Penny ordered. "I'll call you tomorrow to see how it went."

Before I could say anything, she hung up the phone, leaving me speechless and confused. There was no way I could seduce Braxton. He wouldn't even be around me more than five or ten minutes. I slipped my phone into my pocket and climbed the stairs of the bus to find Cash typing away on his computer.

"Hey, Abby." Lane excused himself and left us alone, giving some excuse about checking the venue again. I'd found out that our three new members were a part of a security company that provided protection for some very big names in the music business.

"Hey, Cash," I greeted, pulling a water from the fridge. I slid into the seat across from him at the table and took a drink.

"He's okay." Cash answered the question I was tossing around in my head.

"Is he?" I pushed for more information.

"Yeah, Abby, he is." Cash sighed, closing his laptop. I waited for the handsome bassist to say something, but all he did was steeple his fingers and press them to his lips as he looked off into nothingness. "Are *you* okay?"

"Me?" I squeaked, unsure of why he was asking about me and not telling me anything about Braxton.

"Yeah, you," he replied with a hard stare. "This cannot be easy on you."

"I really wish everyone would quit with the poor Abby shit," I complained, making Cash sit up straighter from my outburst. "Sorry."

"No need to be sorry," he chuckled. The corner of his lip lifted into a smile. If I didn't love Braxton, I'd probably swoon just from that look. The bassist was very good looking, and I could see why a lot of the females gravitated toward him.

"I'm really fine, Cash," I promised, letting my shoulders slump. "I know you know what happened between us."

"Parts of it," Cash replied, never looking away from me. He kept eye contact, and that was refreshing, because when people found out about my scars, their eyes would always bounce around like they were trying to see them. It was a morbid fascination, and one a lot of people couldn't help, but it still bothered me. "Braxton doesn't tell us much."

"I'll tell you," I began, but Cash held up his hand for me to pause.

"Abby, you don't have to tell me."

"You should know," I said, then shrugged. "It's in the past, even if Braxton can't forget, or forgive, himself."

"I'll listen, but only if you want to tell me." Cash leaned back in the seat, relaxing his body language.

"Braxton and I had been dating for a long time," I began, smiling when I remembered those days. "His old band was booked on a six week tour, and I was happy for him. I really was, but when he came home, he was different. He looked different and acted like another person."

The day he came home was so hard on us. He didn't want to see me, and I forced myself to go to his house, but he wasn't there. When I finally saw him three days later, I knew something was off.

"Go ahead," he urged, after I had paused for several seconds.

"God, he was so messed up. He couldn't concentrate and his body had shrunk in size, not that he was super huge back then, anyway. It was about two months after he came home that we went out on a date. He was late by almost an hour. When we got on the highway, I noticed the needle marks in his arm. I asked him what they were, even though I knew in the back of my mind what was going on. I just didn't want to admit it to myself. Well, we argued, and I tried to touch his arm, and that's all I remember."

"The wreck?" Cash asked.

"Yeah," I nodded. "I woke up from a coma weeks later. Braxton had been arrested, and I was burned down the left side of my body. My mother gave me a letter he'd hand written, letting me go."

"Have you seen him since then?" Cash pushed, reaching out to touch my hand when I wiped away a tear. "It's okay, Abby. You don't have to talk about it."

"I saw him about a year ago, but he wouldn't talk to me." I shrugged. "I found out about six months ago that my bills were being paid by an anonymous person. My mother had hidden it well from me. Well, I didn't have to wonder who it was, because I knew it was him."

"He harbors a lot of guilt over you," Cash informed me.

"He shouldn't," I growled, making a fist that I wanted to slam down on the table, but I didn't. I kept my composure. "Do you know that he lives in a studio apartment in a horrible part of town?"

"Yeah," Cash frowned. "He always said that he didn't need anything else since he was always on tour."

"It's because he's broke from paying my bills," I offered, feeling my anger spike. "I have insurance, but none of it's being used."

"Damn," Cash cursed, wiping a hand over his face. "I'm so sorry, Abby. I wish I could knock some sense into him, but he has a hard fucking head."

"You're so very right about that," I giggled, feeling a little better after getting that off my chest.

"It's all going to work out." Cash smiled at me. "He's stubborn as a mule, but he loves you. We all see it."

"I wish Braxton saw it," I whispered, sliding out of the seat. "I need some time alone. I'm sorry, Cash."

With that, I found my way back to my bunk and climbed in, pulling the curtain tight.

Chapter 21
Braxton

The crowd roared as we finished the first song. I grabbed a bottled water, downing it as quickly as possible before tossing it behind me. Liam was off the side of the stage watching us, and I frowned, because he should have been out front with Abby. I made a motion for him to come up behind my kit where he couldn't be seen when the lights dimmed.

"Where's Abby?" I yelled over the crowd.

"Out front, why?" he replied, kneeling low. I heard Taylor start the next song, and I grabbed my sticks, shaking my head at Liam.

"She better not be alone!"

"Lane is with her," he promised, causing my head to pound. I liked Marshall and Hayden, but the new guy made me want to kill a motherfucker. He'd stared at Abby's scars too long, and I'd caught him, more than once, checking out her ass.

"Go. Check. On. Her!" I yelled.

Liam's eyes widened and he scurried off the stage as I started to play. I couldn't see him after that, and the next forty-five minutes were torture. I busted my knuckle and broke more sticks than usual. I probably sounded like shit, but I really didn't care. I was worried about her.

As soon as the lights went down on the last song, I was off my stool and down the stairs from the stage, grabbing a towel from Coraline. I started toward the front of the building, but a small hand clamped down over my wrist.

"You can't go barging out there," Caroline warned. "She's fine. I just checked on her."

"She's alone," I replied.

"No, she's not," our tour manager sighed. "Kevin is keeping her company, and Lane is close enough if things get crazy."

"Shit." I collapsed on a stool and wiped my face with the towel again. I'd hidden from her for the past few days, hoping it would get her out of my mind, but all it did was make my obsession with making love to her again all that much stronger.

We couldn't have a relationship again. She was sent to this world as my own personal seductress. I was powerless against her, and my fucked up mind couldn't let her go. I swear, I tried….I really tried to shake her hold on me, but she was in my veins like the drugs that almost took her life and mine.

"Braxton," Cash barked, leaning over to get into my face. "Outside...now!"

"What the fuck, Cash?" I growled, standing up to push him out of my space.

"I've had it with your shit, man," he replied, his face turning red with anger. "Outside. We need to talk."

"Man, fuck you," I retorted, feeling backed into a corner.

"You have five seconds," he continued. Taylor and Ace rushed up behind him and placed their hands on his shoulders, trying to pull him back, but my bassist wasn't having that. He shrugged them off and took another step toward me.

"Guys! Guys!" Coraline barked. "Not here. Get the fuck out to the bus!"

"Coraline, get outta here," Taylor ordered, moving so he was between me and his wife when she moved too close. I wouldn't do anything to hurt her, and they should know that by now. As much of an asshole as I could be, the last thing I would ever do is put a female in a situation where she'd get hurt.

Taking a deep breath, I moved away from Cash and turned on my heel, marching out the door. I heard everyone on my tail, but I didn't say anything until we were on the bus. When the door closed, I spun around and pointed my finger at all of them.

"Do not get in my face again," I warned.

"You need someone to kick your ass," Cash cursed. "How could you treat Abby like that?"

"You know nothing about this," I replied, standing my ground.

"I fucking know," Cash spat. "I know everything. She told me today. How could you treat her like that after she already forgave you?"

"She *told* you?" I replied, dropping my ass onto the couch. "Why does everyone want to talk about it? God knows I don't want to talk about it."

"And let it eat you alive?" Cash continued. "That woman loves you. She's loved you for the past three years, and all you've done is run from her."

"It's not easy seeing her," I exploded, returning to my feet. "Every time I look at her, I see the scars. I did that to her!"

"No, you didn't," a soft voice said from the front of the bus. Everyone turned to see Abby standing there, her eyes wet with tears. "I was partially to blame, Braxton. Why can't you accept that?"

Abby stood there, looking like every man's fantasy. She'd worn black leggings and a beige shirt that hung off of her undamaged shoulder. The left side was long and it covered up her scarring. It broke my heart that she had to wear certain styles of clothes so people wouldn't stare at her. Then, it killed me because I knew she wore that so I wouldn't have to look at them, too.

"We will leave you two to talk," Cash whispered as he turned away. I didn't miss the hard glare he made over her shoulder aimed at me as he left the bus.

"Abby..." I began, but she walked up to me and shoved my shoulder, sending my ass into the seat.

"No, Braxton," she growled, climbing on my lap. My cock instantly hardened at her aggressiveness. I'd never seen that before, and I liked it...a lot. "Damn it! What can I do to make you see that I don't blame you?"

"Nothing," I breathed, my hands clasping onto her hips. My cock and hands had a mind of their own as I pulled her closer to my erection. "Fuck, you are a seductress."

"No," she blushed, ducking her head. When those long, blonde locks of hair fell to cover her face, I used one hand to push them away and cup her cheek. "I can't seduce you."

"You do it every time you are near me," I replied.

"No, I don't," she argued.

"You don't realize it, but your voice is like a siren's call to me," I admitted, taking my thumb and stroking her bottom lip. I relished in the softness. "Your scent is the most expensive perfume."

"Stop, Braxton," she begged. "I don't want to hear your confessions if you are not going to accept my love for you anymore."

"What I say is true," I admitted.

"I'm sorry," she said, backing away. I reached out for her when she stumbled awkwardly to her feet, but she pushed my hands away. "I refuse to be pushed and pulled by your emotions. The only thing I ask is that you forgive yourself. Please?"

"I'm trying," I admitted, feeling my heart shatter even more.

Chapter 22
Abby

I pulled on a pair of sweatpants that hung low on my hips and a long sleeved sweatshirt that barely covered my bellybutton. It was cold out, and we were heading toward to Chicago, where the road conditions were making the trek slow. We still had several hours before we were set to arrive. Their show wasn't until the next day, and Hank, the driver, informed us that he was going to get us in place as safely as possible.

Braxton was coming around. We were going to stop for lunch in a town that I couldn't even remember the name. The only thing I focused on was that he'd asked me if I'd like to go have a bite to eat with him, and I said yes. We needed some time alone.

I grabbed my bag and opened the door leading to the front sitting area of the bus. He was there, waiting on the couch. When I walked forward, he frowned. "What?"

"You're going to freeze out there," he growled, standing up to remove his leather jacket. "Wear this."

"You know that won't fit me," I replied, rolling my eyes.

"Do you have a jacket?"

"Yes," I sighed, returning to my bunk. I grabbed my thick hoodie and slipped it over my head, returning to him. I held my hands out to the side and raised a brow. "Is this okay?"

"It'll do," he mumbled.

Coraline, Taylor, Ace, and Cash all emerged from the back as soon as the bus came to a stop. Our new security team was already at the front of the bus, waiting for us to make our decision. There were three restaurants within walking distance, and I eyed the small diner about the time Coraline begged for her man to take her to the steakhouse.

"Where do you want to eat?" Braxton asked. I knew he wanted us to be alone, and from the look on his bandmates faces, I figured they already knew we wouldn't be going with them.

"The diner looks great," I answered.

"Lane can go with you to the diner," Hayden announced, slipping his phone back into his pocket.

"I think I can take care of Abby on my own," Braxton growled. The sound was predatory, and the look on Lane's face told me he knew Braxton wasn't going to budge.

"We will be close," he stated, his voice clipped with frustration.

"Watch your step folks," our driver called out. "There's some ice on the roads already."

"Cora," Taylor growled as she bound down the stairs. "Damn it, woman! Watch where you're going."

Coraline let out a curse as he picked her up, cradling her pregnant body against his chest. Cash and Ace followed, giving her an equal lashing.

"She's a spitfire," I giggled.

"That she is." Braxton smiled. I knew he thought highly of her, and I'd even noticed how he watched over her like he did Penny.

"Let's go eat," I said, changing the subject. "I'm starving."

"Come on," he said, taking the lead. I followed him, smiling to myself when he held up his hand for me to take it. Hank was right. There were patches of ice on the parking lot, but mostly where the potholes had frozen over.

Braxton didn't release my hand until we entered the diner. A waitress sat us at a table in the back and handed over two menus, promising to be back shortly to take our order. I peeked over the top of mine and found him staring at me. I averted my eyes and tried to scan the menu, finding I couldn't quite read the words.

I was nervous. It wasn't a real date, but it was a date nonetheless. Oh, who was I kidding? We were on a date, and his sister's words were bouncing around in my head. Seduce him? I wasn't the seductress he accused me of. I didn't know how to be sexy for him. It'd always been so easy before. Now, I just felt awkward.

"What can I get you?" the waitress asked as she approached the table. Her eyes scanned his multitude of tattoos, and she looked at me with a weird expression on her face. She raised a brow at me, and I rattled off an order for a salad and some water.

"Steak and eggs," Braxton replied when she asked him.

I folded my hands on the table top and took a deep breath, because we were alone in the corner, and I figured it was a good time to talk things out. "I want to put the past behind us."

"I've tried, Abby," he said sadly, wiping a hand over his face. It was a nervous tick he had and I was fairly sure he didn't even realize he was doing it.

"What can I do? What can I say, Braxton?" I begged, reaching out to take his hand. I felt a small bit of relief when he didn't pull away from me.

He started to speak, but paused when his thumb brushed over the rough patch of scarring on the back of my left hand. I tightened my hold, because I didn't want him to let me go. What surprised me was when he carefully lifted my hand to his lips. I saw the tears well up in his eyes when he pressed a kiss to the scar. "I did this, and for as long as I live, I will never forgive myself."

"I forgive you," I stated, my voice strong and stern. I knew he felt the harshness of my words because he looked up at me with wide eyes. "Now, I am not going to say it again, Braxton Keller. You *have* to stop this before the guilt kills you."

"It's hard." He paused, carefully placing my hand back on the table. I found comfort in the fact that he didn't release his connection. "I don't deserve you, Abby."

"Yes, you do, Braxton," I replied, feeling tears prick the back of my own eyes. "I'll always be your Abby."

"Yes, you will," he nodded. As the waitress returned with our food, a small smile appeared at the corner of his lips and I felt my heart burst open with relief.

I was finally getting through to him.

Braxton tucked into his food while I poured ranch dressing over my salad, picking out the tomatoes. He chuckled and shook his head, silently remembering my hate of the vegetable. Or was it a fruit? Didn't matter, anyway. I hated them. Just like old times, he reached over with his fork and stole them from where I'd piled them on one side of the bowl. I smiled and took a bite, refusing to comment.

"So, be honest with me," Braxton finally spoke up about halfway through our meal.

"What?" I asked.

"Are you really enjoying this job?" His narrowed gaze told me he would be watching for my answer, and heaven knew that man could tell when I was lying, but I wasn't lying when I answered.

"I didn't think I would like it after the first few shows, but it's grown on me." I shrugged, setting my fork on the table. "I like it, now."

"Is it too much for you?" he continued. "It's not bothering your arm, is it?"

"Actually," I started, stretching my scarred arm out for him to see. I didn't uncover it, but I wanted him to know I wasn't ashamed of what happened. "I actually feel really good. Liam won't let me lift anything too heavy. So, I usually just organize after he brings in the boxes."

"Good," he grunted. "He's doing his job."

"I wish I could do more." I frowned. "Maybe, after this heals more, I can be of better use."

"You are doing just fine," he promised, taking my hand again. "I don't want you doing too much, Abby."

"You still care for me," I stated, softening my voice.

"I never stopped," he replied, but his face fell. I knew the moment his memories starting rushing back from the stiffness to his hands. Immediately, I began to rub circles over the back of his hand with my thumb, hoping that would calm him.

"Braxton, please don't," I whispered. "Please don't go to that dark place."

"Are you done?" he asked, clearing his throat. "We need to get back."

"Yeah," I nodded, taking the napkin off my lap and crumbling it before tossing it on top of the table. I stood from my seat, calming my erratic heart.

He took my hand and dropped two twenties on the table to pay for our meal, leaving a healthy tip for our waitress. Outside, the cold wind blew in my face, tossing my hair all around. Braxton stopped and pulled my hair back, tucking it into the back of my hoodie. I smiled and whispered a thank you as he took my hand and walked toward the bus. By the time we climbed the steps, the snow had started and the driver was looking at his phone with a frown.

"Weather is getting bad in Chicago," he informed us. "We will probably make it as far as Joliet before we will have to stop for the night."

Hayden, Marshall, and Lane were searching their phones for weather updates. Each one of them looked grim, and I felt my stomach drop. The food I'd just eaten was now soured.

A hush fell over the bus as he began the trek. I clasped my hands in front of me and tried to shake off the bad feeling I had in my gut. Taylor pulled Coraline down next to him on the small loveseat that sat directly across from us. Liam,

Josh, and Kevin cleaned up the small kitchen area and took their seats at the dinette table. Ace and Cash excused themselves to the living area in the back of the bus with our security team in tow, holding their computers and phones close to their chests.

"I'm going to check in with *Bleeding Secrets*," Ace said as he disappeared past the bunks.

Each bump and turn on the road caused my anxiety to increase, and I knew Braxton felt it from the stiffness of my body. He tried to relax and lean back on the couch. When I didn't follow him, he sat up and wrapped an arm around my waist. "Everything will be okay."

"I know," I sighed. "I just hate driving anywhere in the snow."

I'd lived in Seattle my entire life, but I never left the house during the worst of any weather. We didn't get snow like they had in Chicago. So, I was a little on edge. I probably looked like an idiot for being nervous, but as I glanced at everyone else, they looked just as worried as I felt.

I decided to look out the windows, breathing a sigh of relief when I noticed there was only a thin layer of snow on the roads. The grass had more of the white stuff, but so far, everything looked fine.

"I need something to do," Coraline announced. "Who wants to watch a movie?"

"That sounds like a damn good idea," Taylor agreed. His eyes connected with Braxton's and I saw something pass between them. I didn't know if that look was a good thing or not, but I would trust them. At this point, it was all I could do, or I'd have a panic attack.

"Comedy," Braxton blurted when Taylor stood up from his seat. There was a television on a partition behind the driver's seat. Within a few minutes, we were set up, and Taylor dimmed the lights before taking his wife back into his arms and holding her protectively.

Braxton finally relaxed and crossed his ankle over his knee. I grabbed a small throw pillow from the other end of the couch and slid down so I could lay down on my side. I didn't even bother trying to put the pillow in his lap. That was too intimate, and with everyone around, I wasn't sure how he'd handle it. I was shocked when he tugged on the pillow under my head. When I lifted my head, he placed it on his lap, and I stifled a smile as I found a new place to rest my head. "Do you want a blanket?"

"No, thank you," I said, then blushed. "I'm fine."

Coraline was curled up in Taylor's lap. It didn't take her long to fall fast asleep. He sat as still as possible, watching the movie in silence so she could sleep. I felt a longing in my heart for that. It'd been so long since Braxton and I had shared special moments. I honestly thought it'd never happen again.

He wasn't touching me, and I wanted so badly to reach up and take his hand, but I didn't. I yearned for him to touch me as tenderly as Taylor touched Coraline. I had to stop myself several times from tucking my hand under the pillow just so I could rest my hand on his muscular thigh.

Ace and Cash never returned from the back of the bus. The rest of the crew stayed close as we continued down the road. It seemed like days before we reached the town of Joliet. I wasn't sure how much further we were from the hotel, but at least we were closer than a few hours ago. I'd be glad when the bus was sitting still for once.

One second, we were sitting at a red light, the next, the bus started through the intersection, but didn't make it far before the driver screamed out, "*Hold on!*"

Braxton's arms were like steel bars as they wrapped around my body, and the next thing I knew, he was taking me to the ground as something crashed into the side of the bus where we had been sitting. Pain lashed the side of my face as my head cracked against the ground. I sucked in a harsh breath, feeling the cold air from outside invade my lungs. A hard shiver rolled through my body as I tried to move. My name was called, but my ears were ringing so badly, I wasn't quite sure who'd said my name.

"Abby!"

"Abby!"

My eyes cleared and I saw a blurry image of Braxton's face. His hands touched the side of my face, holding me in place. I shivered again and mumbled, "C...cold."

"Don't move them!" Someone was yelling for help. Maybe it was Ace? Cash? At that point, I was just too tired to care. When I heard the voice again, I realized it was Hayden.

I was so tired. Braxton's warmth around me felt amazing. Why was the air turned on anyway?

"Don't you dare go to sleep, Abby," Braxton ordered. "Open your eyes. Look at me!"

I tried to pry my eyes open and saw his beautiful blue ones staring at me, and for a moment, I found myself lost in them, thinking they were back to the vibrant blue I'd remembered from so long ago. He was so handsome. As my mind started to clear, I tried to reach up and touch my head, but Braxton grabbed my hand, pulling it back to my side. "No, don't touch your head, baby girl."

"It hurts, and I'm cold," I complained, finally blinking away the haze over my eyes. When I got a good look at Braxton, there was a trail of blood leading from his hairline down between his eyes and around his nose. "You're hurt!"

"I'm fine," he said, still leaning over me. "It's just a cut."

"But you're bleeding," I pointed out, but was cut off when he pressed his finger to my lips.

The blood wasn't dripping off of his chin yet, and I took his words as truth, but seeing him hurt had tears building in my eyes. Braxton's eyes widened and he leaned closer so we were nose to nose. "An ambulance is on its way. You took a hit to the head, and you are bleeding, too. I don't want you to move until they get here just in case you are hurt worse than it looks. Don't cry, Abby."

"Braxton," Lane barked as he came into view. "Let me have a look at your head."

Braxton's gaze rose up momentarily, but he quickly turned it back on me. He growled when Lane pushed on the spot at his hairline. "Check on Abby. I'm fucking fine!"

Lane frowned, but handed Braxton a white rag of some sort to press to his head, and in true Braxton fashion, he tossed it to the side so he could have both hands free. As much of a pain in the ass as he could be, Braxton was always loyal to his friends, putting their needs above his own. Just look at what he'd been doing for the last three years by living in squalor so my bills would be paid.

"Abby, where do you hurt?" Lane took to my left side, careful of my arm.

"Just my head," I moaned when a pain flared behind my right eye. "I'm sure I'm going to be sore in the morning."

"I think we all are," he teased, giving me a weak smile. He looked up at Braxton and whispered something I couldn't quite hear because of the ringing in my ears. On Braxton's nod, Lane moved out of my line of sight.

"You're going to be okay," Braxton said as he leaned over me once again. He was so close that our noses were dangerously close to touching. As stupid as it sounded, I wanted nothing more than for him to press his lips to mine, sealing his promised words that everything was okay. "We will get you to a hospital quickly."

"Stay with me?" I asked, feeling my tears roll out of my eyes. Braxton wiped them away as each one fell. "Don't leave me, Braxton."

"I won't leave your side, Abby. I promise," he whispered, tears welling up in his own eyes. "I won't leave you this time."

There was a commotion behind me. Ace, Cash, and our security team were mumbling, but their words sounded rushed. My mind started taking roll. *Where was everyone?*

"Oh, God!" I gasped now that my brain was finally back online. "Coraline! Where's Coraline?"

"She's okay." He swallowed hard, taking a moment to look over my head. I didn't hear her or anyone else for that matter. "Taylor has her."

"The baby?" I cried. *Please let their baby be okay.*

"I'm sure she will need to be looked at, too," Braxton stated after a long pause. "I think she's okay, just in shock. We all are."

Sirens sounded, cutting off our words. For the longest time, we all quieted as the realization hit us that we'd just been in an accident. I tried to calm my fear every time I saw most of the band and crew moving around us. The most activity was from our security team, and that worried me more than anything else, because of Coraline. They were quiet, but there was also an urgency to all of their movements.

The sound of heavy boots had Braxton looking toward the front of the bus. I heard Taylor's frantic voice, "My wife is twenty-two weeks pregnant. She says her back hurts."

My heart shattered, tears poured from my eyes, and when I tried to look behind me, Braxton held my face again. "She's going to be okay."

"But…" my voice trailed off when he shook his head.

"Ma'am," a man said as he knelt at my side. "Do you hurt?"

"Just my head," I replied, feeling a constant dull pain above my ear.

"We are going to get you looked at," he told me, reaching into his bag to retrieve his supplies. While they put a neck brace on me, I watched as another paramedic tended to Braxton. His eyes never left mine, and I found some comfort in the fact that he was there. He wasn't freaking out. In fact, he was the epitome of calm, and I hoped that was a good thing.

I was put onto a backboard and moved to a stretcher. Braxton insisted on riding in the ambulance with me, and they agreed. The ride to the hospital was slow, but we made it through the snow that had started falling right after the accident.

"Sir, we will need to take a look at that wound," a nurse said as Braxton walked alongside my stretcher. "I'll need you to come with me."

"No," he growled, ignoring the woman. He was still watching me, and I raised my hand from its place on the gurney, laying it on his hand that had a death grip on the rails. "Braxton, go with her. I'll be fine."

"No."

"Braxton, go with her," I scolded, turning to the nurse. "He can come to me when he gets checked out, right?"

"Yes, ma'am," she said with a smile. "I want to look at that cut to see if it needs stitches, and I'll bring him to your room as soon as we are done."

"Go with her, Braxton," I said, closing my eyes. "I'll be okay."

He didn't reply, just let go of the hold he had on the stretcher. The paramedics kept rolling me away as he stood there in the hallway of the emergency department. The nurse spoke softly to him and he nodded, following her into another room.

A doctor met us as I was placed in my own room. He introduced himself and grabbed my chart. He went over all of the information he had, asking me questions. After I gave him my history and told him that I wasn't allergic to anything, he ordered some scans of my head.

"Someone will come get you shortly," he replied. "I'm going to go check on your friends."

"What about Coraline?" I asked, accepting help from another nurse who elevated the head of the bed I was on so I could at least sit up.

"She's seeing another doctor, but I'll check in on her for you," he promised, closing the door softly.

The next hour, I was taken back for all kinds of tests to make sure I hadn't cracked my head open. Braxton was waiting on me by the time I returned. He was sporting a few stitches where he'd been cut. "Are you okay?"

"Yeah, just some glass cut my head." He paused, taking a deep breath. "I'm more worried about you."

"I'm sure I am fine," I replied, hoping like hell I didn't have some crazy concussion or something.

"Are you hurting still?" he asked, walking over to the bed.

"No." I smiled, scooting over as far as I could so he could sit on the edge of the bed. "It just throbs a little."

We were interrupted by the doctor. I blew out a harsh breath in relief when he came in with a smile on his face. "Everything looks normal. I'm going to release you, but suggest you rest for a few days. Take some Tylenol for any headaches, and if it gets worse, please come back here as soon as possible. The nurse will give you your release instructions."

"Thank you," I replied, trying to stay strong in front of Braxton. I knew he was on the verge of losing control. I could see it in his eyes and I worried he'd run from me again if I was hurt.

I rolled my head to the left and saw him staring intently at me, but he wasn't looking at my face. No, Braxton was staring at my left arm that was exposed from wearing a short sleeved hospital gown.

It was the first time he'd seen my scars in the bright light, and from the hard set to his jaw, I knew he'd just recessed back into his self-imposed journey to hell for the damage he'd caused me.

"Braxton, don't leave," I said as he stood and marched out the door.

Chapter 23
Braxton

"How's Coraline?" I asked as soon as I reached the waiting room.

"We haven't heard anything yet." Cash cursed, standing up from his seat. "Taylor came out about half an hour ago to let us know that they were going to run some tests on her and the baby. How's Abby?"

"She's okay," I answered, trying to forget the vision of her scarred arm. Although we'd made love since this tour started, the room had been dark and I hadn't been focused on anything but reliving the past and what we'd had all those years ago.

"You doing alright?" Cash interrupted my thoughts.

"No," I grunted, holding up my hand when Cash started to say something, but he still voiced his opinion.

"She needs you and you need her," he replied, but I just wanted to change the subject.

"What about the guy that hit us?" I asked, knowing the man had some injuries, but I didn't know how severe they were, and I needed to get the questions off of myself and Abby.

"He didn't make it." Ace cursed, overhearing our conversation. "The police said the man was intoxicated."

"Damn," I growled, dropping into the seat next to him.

Why did I fucking run out of that room? Why did seeing her scars up close hit me with a flood of everything we'd shared and everything we'd lost? I couldn't keep doing this to myself. She was in that room, injured, and I couldn't even stay there to hold her hand while she was released. How much of an asshole had I become?

Fuck! I felt like the worst of human beings. I loved that woman. I'd loved her since the day she came into my life. Had it really been five years? She was barely twenty-one when I'd met her at a small little bar my old band had played at on a Saturday night.

Abby had accepted me, flaws and all, but I pushed her away. I'd almost killed her and she forgave me for every mistake I'd made. I was killing myself by fighting the inevitable. I couldn't imagine her with another man, and I sure as hell couldn't imagine myself with another woman. I hadn't even entertained another woman in three years. There was no one else for me…except Abagail Hampton.

"The bus is not drivable," Cash announced as he hung up his phone. "Hank is on the phone with the rental company, trying to get us something by morning. I'm securing us a hotel close by, and we can stay there until tomorrow."

"Why don't you all go to the hotel?" Ace said, standing up to stretch. "I'll stay here until there is word on Coraline."

"I don't want to leave Coraline," Abby spoke up as she entered the waiting room, tilting her head so she could look into my eyes. "Please, Braxton. Can we stay?"

"You need to rest," I replied, seeing the dark circles forming under her eyes. The thought of Abby possibly being uncomfortable didn't sit well with me. I noticed she was holding her left arm close to her side. I stood up from my seat and walked right up to her, knowing I looked like I was raging mad, but I had to know. "How's your arm?"

"Stiff, but I think that's from the tumble I took." She paused, looking uncomfortable.

"We have hotel rooms," I said. "We should get you over there."

I heard her let out a soft yawn, and I was about to tell her that we should go to the hotel when the doors to the emergency room opened and Taylor exited, his eyes swollen with tears. His expression was one I'd seen before. It was damn similar to the night he found out Coraline had lost their first child.

"Oh, Taylor," Abby cried out, rushing to his side.

"It's…it's a girl," he choked out, wrapping an arm over Abby's shoulders. "The ultrasound tech said I had a healthy baby girl."

"Coraline's okay?" Ace asked, reaching out to put his hand on Taylor's shoulder. I did the same when our guitarist swayed. Ace and I walked him over to a seat and pushed him down. "Is Coraline okay?"

"Yeah." He smiled, looking up at us with a huge grin. "Everyone is fine."

"Thank God." Abby slumped into a seat, tears pouring from her eyes. By that time, we were all tired, sore, and in need of some good news.

"They're going to release us, but Coraline is on bed rest for the next few days." He chuckled. "She's so fucking pissed."

"I bet she is," Ace replied, but my mind was focused on Abby. She was still crying to herself.

"Hey," I said, kneeling at her feet. "She's going to be okay."

"I know," she sniffled. "I'm sorry…I just…with the wreck…and the baby…and…and…"

"I know." I didn't know what else to say to her.

Taylor told us all to go get some rest and he'd talk to us the next day. Cash came in with our new bodyguards and handed out room keys to the hotel around the corner. I followed Abby out to the rented SUV and helped her inside. I didn't sit in the back with her, preferring to put as much distance between us as possible. Lane slipped into the driver's seat and gave me a sideways glance as he started the vehicle.

I couldn't keep putting Abby into these situations. The accident was the second time she'd been hurt in my care, and it needed to end. My sanity was wearing thin, and I couldn't concentrate with her around. The worry was slowly driving me insane. My love for her would be never ending, but I knew what I had to do.

"Here's your key," I offered when we arrived at the hotel. "Go on up and get some rest." Abby slid out of the back seat and took the key, staying silent as she walked away.

"Everything alright?" Lane asked as he crossed his arms over his chest.

"I need you to get Abby a flight back to Seattle first thing in the morning," I ordered. "I'm firing her so she can return home."

"What?" Cash barked as he approached. I didn't even realize he'd hopped into another SUV with Hayden. His blond hair fell into his angry eyes as he approached me, grabbing my shirt in his fist. "Have you lost your fucking mind?"

"Not here," Hayden barked, rushing up to our side.

"Here is perfectly fine," Cash snapped. "You are an asshole, Braxton Keller."

"She needs to go home," I replied, running a hand down my face. I knew I was an asshole, but I was also looking out for Abby.

"Get into your hotel rooms and calm the fuck down." Hayden pulled Cash away from me and spoke softly to him before sending my bassist in through the doors. I looked around and saw both guards standing nearby, watching me like I was going change my mind.

"Do it," I growled, turning on my heel to follow Cash inside. "Send her home on the first plane out tomorrow."

Chapter 24
Abby

The scenery passed outside the SUV as I stared out the window, completely in shock at what I had been told that morning. Marshall had come to my room to tell me I was being let go and my bags had been retrieved from the wrecked bus. With a sad sigh, he told me they were awaiting me in the SUV.

I pushed away each tear that leaked from my eyes, but I kept my cool and didn't voice my anger. I knew what had happened, and I didn't need a fucking note to read his bullshit excuses. The goodbye note I received with my termination sat on the seat next to me, still in an envelope with the hotel's logo on the outside corner.

My head still throbbed from the bump I'd taken during the accident. Thankfully, I didn't have a concussion or anything serious. At least I was awake this time when he left me.

"Fuck," I growled under my breath. I looked up and saw Marshall look in the rearview mirror with concern. I just shook my head and returned to staring out the window.

When we finally arrived at the airport, I was surprised when the bodyguard parked the SUV in the long-term parking lot instead of just dumping me at the curb. When he opened my door, all he said was, "I'm flying to Seattle with you to make sure you arrive safe and sound."

"I don't need to be babysat," I barked, jerking my right arm from his hold.

I reached back to grab the note Braxton had sent along with me and turned to the guard. Tearing it up into as many tiny pieces as I could, I grabbed Marshall's wrist and dropped the pile in his hand, closing his fingers around the remains. "You can return this to Braxton instead of holding my hand while I fly home."

"My job is to see that you make it home safely," he repeated, looking down at his hand.

I ignored him and retrieved my two bags from the back of the SUV, not waiting on him to help. Slinging my backpack over my shoulder, I looked up when he tried to follow me. "I'd advise you to get back in that truck and leave me be."

"Abby," he said, his eyes narrowing. "My job…"

"Fuck your job," I replied, wiping away a tear. "And fuck Braxton Keller."

"You're not going to Seattle alone," he pushed, moving closer to my side.

"If you even *think* about walking with me into that airport, I will make the biggest scene you've ever witnessed."

"Fuck," he swore, his shoulders slumping in defeat. I felt guilty for being a bitch, but I wasn't going to back down.

"I'm sorry, Marshall," I sighed, "but I can take it from here." Without another word, he slid into the driver's seat and drove away.

The cold wind blew my hair as I turned and made my way into the airport. The lines for check-in were long, and I closed off my mind to all thoughts as I waited to get my ticket. I kept my head down as I moved on through security. The lady who checked my ID looked at me with concern, but I was sure she'd seen many travelers with red eyes and runny noses as they left their loved ones behind. My case was so much different.

I was being thrown away…again.

My stomach growled as I waited for my plane to board, but I didn't eat anything. The gnawing at my gut made me more nauseous than anything else. I was afraid if I did eat, I'd be violently sick.

I tried not to think about Braxton, but it was very hard to do when I sat down in my first class seat. He'd done it again, spending needless money on me when I could've taken care of myself. When was he going to stop? Would he ever stop?

What if I found someone else?

That thought brought a whole new round of tears to my eyes, and I used the pillow and blanket provided to me to shield my face from the flight attendant as she walked around preparing the plane for departure. The next few hours in the air were spent with me silently sobbing.

When we arrived, I hurried down to baggage claim to get my suitcase. By that time, I just wanted to return to my apartment and lock the doors for the next few weeks. I was so hurt and angry at him, I didn't want to see anyone.

"Of fucking course," I snarled when I saw a man in a suit holding my name on a whiteboard.

I tucked my chin and walked past him without being noticed. Out on the curb, I flagged down a taxi and quickly spat out my address. He didn't say anything as he loaded my bags and drove away from the Seattle airport.

My heart was in shreds. I'd been given an opportunity to see the world and it was yanked out of my grasp by a man who owned me body and soul. It wasn't his decision, but I was smart enough to leave. As much as I wanted to stay and fight for us, I knew that this accident had broken any chance of there being an *us* to salvage. Braxton had made his choice, and it didn't include me. Any seduction I would've tried with him was bound to have a fatal outcome.

I unlocked my apartment door and tossed my bags on the couch, not caring to unpack or do anything more than crawl into my bed so I could cry myself to sleep.

* * *

The morning was met with bright sun outside my window. I didn't have any energy to walk over to pull the curtains closed. My dreams had been full of scenarios where I actually fought for our relationship and confronted Braxton for sending me home. I kept waking up before the dream was finished.

My phone rang from its place on the nightstand. When I looked at the screen, I saw

Penny's name, and I reached over to press the button to send it to voicemail. The second time it rang, I turned off my phone completely. I didn't want to talk to anyone with the last name of Keller.

Wrapping the blanket from my bed around my body, I shuffled my feet as I made my way into the kitchen, throwing together what I needed for a cup of coffee. My living room windows looked out onto the street, and my goal was the windowsill. It was cold outside, despite the sun, but I didn't care. I just wanted to stare into space and hope that my mind wouldn't stray to the memories I had of him.

I sipped at my coffee and didn't really taste it. My mind wasn't going to give me what I wanted, and I found it a thousand miles away with him. He was hurting, and again, I was the cause of it. The bus accident scared him. I wasn't stupid. I knew exactly why he sent me home. I didn't need a letter to explain it to me, either.

I'd cried so much the night before, I thought I didn't have any more left inside, but I proved myself wrong when I felt the wetness on my cheeks. The difference was the tears before were of sadness…now, they were tears of anger. I'd let him just send me away without a fight.

I should've fought for him, but at that point, it was already over between us.

He'd made the decision for us both.

I saw her car pull up outside. Penny hurried toward my building, and I waited for the buzzer. When she pressed it repeatedly, I ignored her. It wasn't a good idea for her to see me in this condition. If I knew my best friend, she'd give her brother hell for sending me home. I didn't need her to do that, and I sure as hell didn't need her to see me all red faced from crying. It was one thing for the people at the airport who didn't know me, it was another for Penny to witness it.

"*Abagail Hampton!*" Penny blared as she beat her fist on my door.

"Damn, who let her in the building?" I cursed under my breath.

"*Open the damn door!*"

"Go away, Penny," I replied through the door. Resting my forehead against the solid wood frame, I prayed she'd give up, but I knew she wouldn't.

"Let me in," she mumbled. It was so low, I almost didn't hear what she said. "Please, Abby."

I raised my fist and beat it against the frame twice in frustration before I reached for the deadbolt. As soon as I threw the lock, Penny pushed her way inside. The moment she took in my features, she dropped her bag to the floor and pulled me into her arms. All I could do was cry into the arms of my best friend as my legs gave out. We fell in a heap on the floor, but she never let me go, staying there until the tears subsided.

"I tried so hard to get him to see how much I loved him, but he sent me away."

Chapter 25
Braxton

A commotion at the backstage gate caused me to turn around to see what was going on as I stepped off the bus. I had to blink a few times to get my brain on board with what I was seeing. Marshall was holding back a woman who was cursing him for all she was worth, using her hands to try to push his massive body to the side. The moment he put his hands on her, I took off at a dead run.

"Get your fucking hands off my sister!" I roared so loudly, everyone stopped in their tracks.

"Yeah, you big behemoth!" Penny barked as Marshall stepped aside.

"This is your sister?" he asked in disbelief. They'd not met yet, and I hadn't even thought to let them know about my family, because I didn't expect any of them to show up this far from home.

"Yes, I'm his sister," Penny replied, sneering at the guard.

"What the fuck are you doing in Louisville?" I grabbed her arm and pulled her toward the bus. Cash came rushing down the stairs and stopped dead in his tracks, repeating what I had said to my sister.

"Well, I'm happy to see you too, brother," she snarled, her sarcasm telling me she wasn't happy at all. "I'm sorry, Cash, but I need to talk to him."

"This is not the time," I warned, feeling my heart ache in my chest. The last few days had been hell on my nightmares. Abby's voice begging me not to leave her in that hospital room was the only thing I'd heard when I let the memories sink through the wall I'd built around my thoughts.

"You need to talk to your sister," Cash said, taking a deep breath, holding his hand out toward the bus. "Go to the bus."

Penny started walking away, not looking at either of us. She was pissed, and I wanted to know how Abby was doing, but I didn't need to ask. Seeing my sister in Kentucky was enough to tell me that things at home were bad.

"She's miserable," Penny said as soon as the doors closed on the bus. "You are the biggest asshole on the face of the planet, Braxton Keller."

"I did what was best," I argued, folding my arms over my chest.

"For Abby?" Penny barked, her face turning red. "God! You are so dense sometimes, Braxton."

"Is she okay?" I finally asked after a moment of silence. I had to know.

"No, she's not okay," she replied. "The only time I've ever seen someone in that much pain was when I looked at you after the first time you left her."

"Every time she is with me, she gets hurt!" I exploded, throwing my hands in the air. "I can't keep doing that to her."

"The accident wasn't your fault," Cash interrupted. "Dude, you have got to stop this shit. It's killing you not to be with Abby."

"Man, fuck you," I snarled, looking at my bassist. "Stay out of this."

"No, fuck you!" he bit back, pointing at my face. "I hear you calling out for her in your sleep at night. I know the nightmares are back, Braxton. We all hear you."

"You have three days off after this show," Penny said, using her finger to poke me in the chest. "I'd advise you to return to Seattle with me and make things right."

"No," I growled. "It's over."

"Who said?" she snapped. "You?"

"Jesus, Braxton," Cash replied, running his hand through his long, blond hair. "She fucking loves you! Why would you throw something like that away? I'd give anything to have someone like that in my life. Maybe I'll call Abby since you are too much of a pussy to accept her."

Blood boiled in my veins at the thought of Cash touching my Abby. Penny shouted out a warning to either Cash or myself, but I didn't care. I launched at him, taking the pretty boy to the ground. My hands bunched up in his shirt as I pulled his face close to mine; our noses touching. "You do *not* touch my Abby!"

"Then you need to claim her and make things right," he ordered, pushing me away to stand again. I fell to my ass and covered my face with my hands. "I don't want your girl, and your actions right now prove to me that you love her. Don't fuck this up for a *third* time."

"Are you ready to go home with me tomorrow?" Penny asked, her left hand resting on her hip…the other one held a phone out in front of her. "Call her, Braxton, and hope like fuck she takes you back."

"She doesn't need me in her life."

"You need her," Cash pushed. "I'd never seen you happy before Abby came on tour with us. Yes, you were still a grumpy asshole, but you smiled a lot more."

"I can't call her." I shook my head and backed away from my sister's outstretched hand. I didn't need to hear Abby's voice, because if I did, I was afraid I'd crumble.

"Then I'll call her for you," Penny offered, pressing a few buttons on her phone.

I heard the ringing on the other end as Penny held the phone loosely to her ear with the volume turned up as high as it would go. It seemed like forever before the line clicked and her voice came over the line. My heart shredded in my chest when I heard her crying.

"What…what is it, Penny?" Abby sniffled across the line.

"Abby," I gasped as I took the phone from my sister. "Baby, are you okay?"

"Braxton?" she whispered. "Where is Penny?"

"She came to Louisville."

"Penny!" Abby cursed on the other end of the line. There was some rustling that sounded like bedsheets being moved and then the line went silent.

"Abby?"

"I'm sorry she came there, Braxton," Abby said softly, a small hiccup breaking her voice. "I can't do this anymore…I'm sorry for everything."

And the phone clicked…ending our call.

"Son of a bitch!" I roared, stopping myself from throwing my sister's phone across the bus. A protective side of me flared; one I hadn't felt in a very long time. My Abby had just apologized for something that wasn't her fault. The pain in her voice set me on edge.

"I need to go home."

"I have a plane ticket already waiting for you," Penny calmly told me, glancing at Cash. He nodded and walked off the bus, leaving us alone.

"When do we leave?"

"At five in the morning," she replied, walking up to me and wrapping her arms around my waist. My sister hugged me tight, whispering, "It's going to be okay, Braxton. Everything is going to be okay."

I didn't realize until then that tears were streaming down my face.

Chapter 26
Abby

I'd never given up on anything in my life…until now.

Braxton was beyond any help I could give him. I'd thought if I could show him how good it'd been all those years ago, he'd snap out of his guilt and anger at what'd happened to me, but I was wrong.

It was early morning, and I pulled a pillow over my head to try and block out any sounds. I needed to sleep. I'd spent the last three nights tossing and turning between bouts of tears. This had to stop. I wasn't a weak woman, but his rejection destroyed me. I had to shake off the pain of losing Braxton again.

A thump outside my bedroom door woke me from my sleep. I jumped from my bed and started toward the door, but screamed when it flew open and a silhouette of a man was standing in the doorway. Fear rushed up my spine, and I made a quick assessment of the items in my bedroom I could use for a weapon. I began to tremble when I found none.

"Abby," Braxton cooed, causing my legs to wobble. It was his voice, but not as harsh as he usually sounded. No, this man's voice was tender. I had to still be dreaming, because Braxton was on tour and he sure as hell wouldn't show up at my apartment just before daybreak.

"Abby," the man repeated, but this time, his voice was edged with worry. I shook my head to clear the cobwebs of the last few days and blinked a few times. When my eyes cleared, I saw him.

"Braxton?"

"I'm sorry," he blurted, moving slowly into the room. He held his hands out like he was a suspect and I was the police. "Please don't cry."

I didn't even know I was crying again. So much for trying to be strong.

"I can't stop," I admitted, using the back of my hand to clear my face.

"Come here," he ordered, reaching out to touch me.

I didn't know what came over me. I'd tried to harden my heart over the past few days, but as soon as his hand made contact with my skin, all reason fled. I rushed to fall into his chest. His scent enveloped me, and I was thankful he was there, because my legs gave out when I broke down, again.

Braxton picked me up and cradled me to his chest, whispering into my hair. I couldn't make out what he was saying, but his deep voice soothed me, quieting the hysterics. As soon as he laid me out on the bed, he stepped back to remove his shoes and shirt. I watched him intently, praying that when I blinked, he wouldn't disappear.

"I've been the biggest asshole in the world," he began, silencing me when I started to argue. He laid down next to me on the bed and cupped my cheek. "Please, forgive me for sending you away."

"I never blamed you for anything," I admitted. I couldn't seem to get wind behind my voice, so I opted for letting him pull me to his chest. His large hand pressed against my head, silently telling me to lay against him.

"I don't know if you can forgive me again. My life isn't complete without you in it. I need you."

"And I need you," I choked out, feeling more tears trail down my face. One splashed onto his chest, but he didn't budge. "But I cannot keep doing this, Braxton."

"Damn it, Abagail," he swore as his voice cracked, using my full name. "I'm sorry for being a complete asshole, and I fucking love you."

"What?" I breathed, tears pooling in my eyes.

"I said…I fucking love you," he replied, taking my lips before I could protest. He kissed me for several minutes before pulling away slowly. "I'm so sorry."

"I love you too, Braxton," I admitted, touching the side of his face. "I've always loved you."

"I want to see you…all of you," he ordered. "It's time I manned the fuck up and faced what happened."

"Braxton," I frowned, "you don't have to do this."

"It's time. I need to see them, Abby," he replied, reaching for my hand. He held it up and examined the scarring in the natural lighting that came from my window. My hands were so tiny compared to his, and the silvery scars stood out in stark contrast to his tanned and tattooed skin. "I think seeing you hurt again jarred my stupid brain into pushing you away. I blamed myself for what happened and thought if I sent you home, you'd be better off, but I was wrong. It took Penny coming to Kentucky to make me see that I needed you. God, I was such an asshole."

"You weren't being an asshole," I replied, closing my eyes. "I understand. I really do."

"It's going to be hard to not feel guilty for the things I've done, but if you will give me another chance, I promise to make you the happiest woman in the world."

"You don't have to do anything but love me to make me happy," I promised. "If you are ready to see me, I will let you, but promise me something?"

"Anything," he nodded.

"Do not run from me again," I replied, as he brushed the hair off my shoulder.

We had to work through this, and I was going to do everything in my power to make things right between us. He had to come to terms with who I was now, and I knew it wasn't going to happen overnight. Braxton needed to face these fears and guilt head on.

"Never," he promised, sliding off the bed. "Let me see you, Abby."

Without hesitation, I reached for the hem of my shirt and lifted it over my head. I knew he saw the milky white skin of my stomach first, because Braxton let out a soft growl. He grew silent when the scars on my left side appeared. I froze for a moment when I realized that he would have a harder time with the ones I kept carefully covered on my arm. With a deep breath, I removed my shirt and tossed it to the floor.

I didn't remove my bra, but I did reached for the button on my jeans next. I knew what I had to do. He swallowed hard when I stood from the bed and seductively removed them by leaning over and slowly sliding them down to my ankles, kicking the material free.

This was the only way I was going to get him to really look at me. Braxton was an alpha male in all ways, and I knew I had to show him that I was still the same woman he knew before the accident. Was I going to seduce him? Yes, yes I was.

"You are beautiful," he said as I righted myself.

"I'm still me," I said, my voice only above a whisper. "I just look different."

"I only see you…my Abby," he said in wonder.

Chapter 27
Braxton

In fact, I didn't even see the scars at first when I looked at her. All I saw was the woman who owned my heart. The Abby I'd fallen in love with many years before. Her slender, yet slightly curvy body called to me, and the scars were just a part of who she was now. It didn't define her like I'd made my mind believe they did for the past three years.

She was just as beautiful with them as she was without.

"God, Abby," I said, dropping to my knees at her feet. My hands clasped onto her hips, and my lips landed on the scars above the waistband of her white lace panties. I placed soft kisses on the ones I could reach, and when I couldn't reach them from my place on my knees, I stood up and made sure I paid attention to every single mark that was on her body.

"Oh," she moaned as I reached her neck. "Braxton."

"Does this make you uncomfortable?" I whispered, nipping her earlobe.

"No," she said, shaking her head just the slightest bit. "It feels so good."

"Touch me, Abby," I demanded softly. "Like you used to."

Her hands clamped onto my shoulders, nails digging into the muscle there. I felt her shiver, and I pulled her body closer to mine. The lace from her bra scratched at my chest, but I didn't remove it. I wanted her to do that.

Those tiny hands caressed me as she continued her exploration. I closed my eyes and let my head fall back on my shoulders when she ran her palms over my chest, stopping to rub circles over my nipples. My cock responded and hardened behind the fly of my jeans.

"You are driving me crazy," I snarled, cupping her face. "I want to make love to you."

"What are you waiting for?" She winked, reaching behind to unhook her bra.

I hooked my fingers into the sides of her panties and pulled them down her legs, stopping to place random kisses on the scars as I knelt again. When I stood upright, her hands returned to my shoulders. Those tiny hands squeezed, and she hummed appreciatively. That sound alone made me want to work out even more to bulk up just so she would touch me like that every single day.

Abby's fingers trailed down over my nipples and she flipped her hands over so she could skim my abs with the backs of her knuckles, stopping at the waistband of my jeans. She made quick work of the button and zipper, reaching in to wrap her hand around my cock.

"Fuck," I moaned as she dropped carefully to her knees, pulling my cock free so she could wrap her lips around it. I locked my knees when she took me to the back of her throat. "Fuck, Abby."

My fingers dug into her hair as I held her face, pumping into her mouth slowly. Those blue eyes I loved to stare into looked up at me with a heated desire that was familiar. When her cheeks hollowed out, I growled low in my throat.

"Do you want me to come in your mouth," I smirked, "or in your pussy?"

A bright red blush covered the tops of her cheeks, and she shifted with the ache I knew was building between her legs. I didn't say anything else as I stroked her chin, silently telling her to release me. When she sat back on her heels, I felt primal again. It was something I hadn't felt in a long time, and I honestly thought I'd never have those desires again.

"On the bed," I ordered, "hands above your head."

"Yes, sir," she whispered, scrambling up to get where I wanted her.

I raised a brow at her when she kept her knees bent but together, hiding her pussy from me. I knew she was going to be a brat by the small smile that played on the corner of her mouth. I wanted to take it further, but at the moment, I just wanted to get lost in her soft touch.

"I'm going to make love to you, my Abby," I said, climbing up on the bed. "Open for me."

My hands shook as she spread her legs, allowing me to climb between them. I took her lips at the same time my cock found its home inside her. We both cursed silently as I began to move. The sensations were intense, and I closed my eyes for a moment when all of the good memories came rushing back in my mind. Her body accepted me and surrounded my cock with her warmth. Sweat beaded up on our skin as we began to find a rhythm. Her moans were soft in the beginning, but within a few minutes, had turned to heated curses. On her next breath, she begged for release.

"Please, Braxton," she begged, digging her nails into my ass as I pounded into her.

"Hold on longer," I ordered, although my demand held no weight.

"I can't," she panted.

My hands cupped her face, pushing a few tendrils of hair off of her forehead. I kissed her lips hard, pumping deep into her body as she screamed out her pleasure. My body tightened and I let go, floating on a high that no needle could provide for me anymore.

"I love you, my Abby," I cried into her neck. Tears fell over my lashes, but I didn't care. The ice around my heart had thawed. I could actually breathe again. The fog that had hung over me for so long was gone. Everything felt right, finally.

"And I love you, my Braxton," she said, wiping away the wetness from my face.

Epilogue
Braxton

My family was here. It was the last night on tour, and I'd flown my mom and sister to New York City for the largest show we'd ever played. There'd been almost fifteen thousand tickets sold, and everyone was pumped for the night.

I pulled a shirt over my head as I exited the bunk area of the bus. My mom was just coming up the steps as I entered the living room of the bus. Her eyes sparked when she saw me smiling at her. "Ma!"

"Oh, Braxton!" she squealed, rushing toward me. I hugged her tight and relished in her scent. It was home and love and everything I'd been fighting for the past three years. "You can put me down, son."

"Sorry." I smiled, reaching out for Penny. She came to me quickly, and I did the same greeting with her I'd done with my mom.

"You look happy," she whispered in my ear.

"I am," I replied, setting her down. "Have you seen my Abby?"

"Actually," my mom blushed, "a handsome young man said he would get her for us."

"That's Marshall." I smiled, feeling better knowing that he'd be looking after Abby when I wasn't around. We'd come to a common understanding: Abby came first in all things. "He's one of our new security guys."

"I don't know how I feel about all of the crazy fans that have been following that *Bleeding Secrets* band," she frowned. "Are you sure it's safe?"

"Mom, we are safe," I promised. "This is the last show, and we will be back home by tomorrow. After that, it's time to write a new album."

"Then you get to do it all over again," Penny cheered. "I'm so happy for both of you, Braxton."

"I'm happy for us, too." I nodded, smiling over my sister's shoulder when I saw Abby walking toward the bus. My mom and sister turned, meeting my girl as soon as she reached the steps.

The women giggled and hugged. It felt great seeing my mom with Abby. They'd always gotten along, and I had a feeling that they had seen each other often when I was away during those three years.

I took a seat at the dinette and watched over the women in my life. I loved them all, and I'd been a complete asshole for far too long. It took me a long time to realize during my self-imposed exile from life, I'd been hurting them as well.

Abby had agreed to return to the tour with me after the three day break when I'd rushed home to Seattle to beg her forgiveness. She'd been miserable, and so had I. Abby was my life, and I'd let my guilt rule me for far too long. Did I forget what happened all those years ago? No, I would never forget the accident that changed my life, because without that, I probably would've been dead from my heroin use. I'd been close to a downward spiral before that fateful night over three years ago, and that accident was the brick wall I'd needed to stop what I was doing to myself and the people in my life.

I pulled Abby over to sit on my lap as my mom and sister made themselves comfortable on the couch. As the women talked, I felt the love they all had, and I realized my family was complete. These women were mine, and I'd failed them for far too long.

"How much time do you have?" Penny asked, looking at the clock on the wall above my head.

"Just enough time to spend with my girls." I grinned, giving Abby's thigh a gentle squeeze.

The End…
Look for Cash's story coming next…

About Theresa Hissong:

Theresa is a mother of two and the wife of a retired Air Force Master Sergeant. After seventeen years traveling the country, moving from base to base, the family has settled their roots back in Theresa's home town of Olive Branch, MS, where she enjoys her time going to concerts and camping with her family.

After almost three years of managing a retail bookstore, Theresa has gone behind the scenes to write romantic stories with flare. She enjoys spending her afternoons daydreaming of the perfect love affair and takes those ideas to paper.

Look for other exciting reads…coming very soon!

Printed in Great Britain
by Amazon